secrets of the
shopping mall

richard peck

secrets of the shopping mall

a yearling book

Published by
Dell Publishing
a division of
Bantam Doubleday Dell Publishing Group, Inc.
666 Fifth Avenue
New York, New York 10103

The trademark Yearling® is registered in the U.S. Patent and Trademark
Office.

The trademark Dell® is registered in the U.S. Patent and Trademark
Office.

ISBN: 0-440-40270-0

Reprinted by arrangement with Delacorte Press

Printed in the United States of America

December 1989

10 9 8 7 6 5 4 3

OPM

For Marcie and Fred Imberman

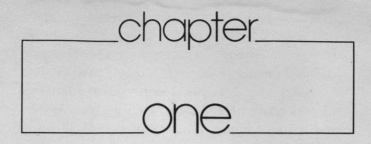

chapter

one

The day had dawned gray and gritty, as usual. The cross-town bus wheezed up to the corner, and Teresa climbed down out of it, two stops away from school. She slouched on in the direction the bus was going, along one of the side streets the other kids seldom used.

Shopping-bag ladies snored on stoops. Rats peered intelligently from garbage cans. A blind-eyed TV set in the middle of the sidewalk looked like it had been dropped from a great height.

"Your basic urban scene," Teresa said to herself, crunching on over the broken glass of the picture tube.

There was a nip in the air, along with a single red maple leaf, somehow swirled in from suburbia. Teresa hitched her Goodwill coat closer around her and watched the leaf dance down a storm drain.

This seasonal touch turned her mind to Basic Math: five weeks of school down; thirty-eight to go till summer vacation. Minus Christmas week and the Friday after Thanksgiving. With luck, a couple of snow days. That makes . . . She was trying to remember how much they knock off for Easter when she realized she'd turned the final corner. The school loomed up across the street.

Teresa slowed. Her stomach shrank and groaned. For breakfast she'd had a handful of M&M's and a half bottle of Yoo-hoo. What with that and the start of another school day her insides were queasy.

She waited, wishing the morning bell would ring before she hit the school yard. To look busy, she checked the coin return in the corner phone booth and dropped an invisible letter in the mailbox. Not that anybody was noticing her. All the action was behind the wire fence around the school, and nobody would notice her even if she was over there.

In fact she had to step off the curb to keep from being run down by Dolores Schwab and Angela Santorelli who seemed unable to see her. She watched Dolores and Angela jaywalking across to the gap in the school fence in matching down jackets, leather-look jeans, and heeled boots. "Must be nice to have friends," Teresa said without moving her lips, a childhood habit that she couldn't quite kick. "Not that I'd necessarily pick either one of those two."

Deep inside the school the morning bell went off,

rattling the window grates. A mean moan rose from the school yard, and groups merged with groups up the smooth school steps. Cigarette butts arched like fireworks into the street. Teresa crossed from gutter to gutter and let herself be swallowed by the mob. She waited, lonelier in the crowd than out of it, for people to stop punching people and start climbing.

The steps were backed up, nobody wanting to be first inside. Nobody wanted to be at the rear either, where the tougher gangs were moving in and spotting for stragglers. Somehow Teresa had been elbowed in between Dolores and Angela, who were talking around her in a language of their own invention. She stared in the air, examining once again the letters above the front door, which now read:

RATSO LUV CHARLEEN JUNIOR HIGH SCHOOL

At one time the school had had either a name or a number, but graffiti had wiped it out. "I am an inmate," Teresa said through unmoving lips, "of the Ratso Luv Charleen Junior High School." And at that, somebody threw a punch at the small of her back, and she was swept into school.

The crowd moved around the top of the stairs to the basement where four guys in black plastic Windbreakers had Billie Novak on his back and were shaking him down for his bus-pass money. Teresa entered the home-room door, which two unenrolled types were trying to lift off its hinges.

The lockers had been moved out of the hall and were at the back of homeroom. Locker doors were already banging open as Teresa reached hers and hurried through her combination. A lot of people always hung around back there talking until the homeroom and social-science teacher, Mrs. DeFalco, started screaming. But Teresa had no one to talk to, so she jammed her coat in and wandered back up the aisle.

It wasn't school itself she minded. It was her loner status. Teresa was forever trying to explain it to herself. She lived with her aunt who was basically a drifter. She'd gone to five elementary schools. Now, in junior high, everybody seemed to have his or her friendships completely nailed down. So for her, going to school was like crashing a party every morning. She pulled her sweat shirt as far down as possible over her stretch slacks and collapsed into a seat.

"Giddoutta there," said Dolores Schwab from the seat across the aisle.

"Who, me?" Teresa said.

"I'm talking to you, aren't I, Lardface?" Dolores inquired, pulling lip gloss and assorted small bottles out of her purse and slamming them down on her desk. "So, giddoutta there." Dolores's plucked eyebrows rose, and her eyes narrowed. "Gid . . . dout . . . ta . . . that . . . seat. You understand English?"

4

"What for?" Teresa asked, finding herself having a conversation at last.

"Because that's Angela's seat is what for. So get the—"

"Since when have we had assigned seats?" Teresa asked, wondering if they'd slipped in another new rule on her.

Dolores gazed at the ceiling, looking for patience. "Angela sits next to me because I say so," she said, not bothering to look at Teresa. "You sit anywhere you can find. Or stand." She drew out a particularly sharp-looking nail file and whipped the air with it.

Teresa looked at the glint on its point and heaved herself up. The only empty seats were at the front as usual. She settled into one directly in front of Mrs. DeFalco's desk just as Mrs. DeFalco rose up behind it screaming, "I want quiet in here!"

"You'll never get it," came a voice from farther back.

Mrs. DeFalco made a grab for her blackboard pointer to slam it down on the desk. But unknown hands had sawed the pointer into four sections and had laid them back down together, so Mrs. DeFalco grabbed up what looked like a twig, which was good for a laugh.

"Now it's time for attendance," she yelled, pitching the twig behind her and planting her hands on the desk. "Is everybody here?"

"More or less," came another voice behind Teresa.

"All right." Mrs. DeFalco swept a wad of hair off her forehead with a hand that held a red ball-point. A fiery red line of ink appeared like a sudden wound below her scalp. Which was good for another laugh. "Now," she roared, "it's time to collect the bus-pass money, so get your—"

The door to the hall, still barely on its hinges, swung open, and the assistant principal filled up the space. His arms were longer than his sleeves, and furry knuckles seemed to graze the floor. A kid in the second row offered him a banana.

"Oh, no," moaned Mrs. DeFalco, clutching her attendance book, "not another one."

The assistant principal nodded and lumbered into the room. At first Teresa thought he was alone, but walking behind him was a very small kid, a boy. He was carrying books, which meant he was new.

"Look," Mrs. DeFalco said to the assistant principal, "I've already got forty of them in here."

He squinted out over the room that was thick with flying objects. "Doesn't look like forty to me, quite."

"What does it *sound* like?" Mrs. DeFalco asked. She was screaming still, but Teresa was reading her lips.

"It sounds like the Korean War," the assistant principal said. "But I got another one for you."

"Discipline case?" Mrs. DeFalco mouthed.

"Naw," said the assistant principal. "Gifted."

"I've heard that one before." The teacher planted a hand on her hip.

"He's a bright little squirt," the assistant principal said. "Name's Barnie. They're moving him up from seven. They figure he'll get more of a challenge in eight."

"How true," Mrs. DeFalco said. Then she whirled on the class. "If there is any more noise in this room, I am going to send the perpetrators back to the office with the assistant principal."

The assistant principal's jaw dropped in horror, and his eyes froze. In two strides he was out the door. The new kid, Barnie, was left standing alone, in a lumber jacket, Levi's, and a pair of small yellow construction boots. Teresa examined him from her post in the front row. He had a somewhat pinched but pleasant face and was giving the teacher a long, direct look.

"Settle down now, class," she bellowed. "We have a new member—Barnie—and I'm sure you'll want to make him welcome."

The class yelled, "Hel-lo, Barn-ieeee," in an evil singsong. Teresa said nothing.

"Sit anywhere, Barnie," Mrs. DeFalco said.

"Sit any-where, Barn-ieeee," the class chanted.

"Where's the rest of him?" asked a deep voice in the back row, and Angela Santorelli cackled a piercing laugh. Barnie edged into the seat next to Teresa. And try as she would, she couldn't even look his way.

The days limped along—cooler, grayer. Teresa got through them as usual. She kept an eye on Barnie too, when he wasn't looking. She'd wanted to say something to him on that first day, but she didn't know what. She

7

wanted to be his friend, but she didn't know what she had to offer.

So she left him alone long enough for him to notice he had troubles of his own: he was too smart for the seventh grade and too short for the eighth. This was enough to peg him as an outcast. And once they've pegged you, they've pegged you for life. This Teresa knew.

She knew a lot, mainly from watching and listening. Since nobody talked to her, she eavesdropped on other people's conversations: girls' conversations when she could get near enough, but mainly boys' since they were louder.

The worst gang of them in her grade was a bunch that called themselves the King Kobras. The leader was Harley Probst, as low a life-form as Teresa had ever encountered. He'd been in family court once on a charge of hotwiring an Olds Cutlass. The truth was he'd hotwired half of General Motors before he hit puberty.

The Kobras were sitting together at the back of Mrs. DeFalco's social-science class, which was last period. Teresa was right in front of them. This time she couldn't have missed hearing if she'd tried.

Harley Probst, who used school only for scheming, had noticed that Barnie was within a couple of inches of being the same size as a wall locker. This could mean only one thing to Harley. And Teresa heard exactly what it meant, though the Kobras didn't notice she was within a mile of them.

When the final bell rang, she joined the stampede

8

back to the lockers. Everybody crowded around with gouging, flying elbows. Combination locks whirred. Books crashed in. Coats billowed out. People made after-school plans with other people.

And Harley Probst's Kobras were coiling up, ready to strike. Barnie's locker was two down from Teresa's, and so she saw the Probst Plan go into action. Barnie had no sooner pulled his locker door open than he was inside, jammed in there by eight fists. They mashed Barnie into his locker and banged the door shut so fast he must have thought he'd been struck blind. Harley stood back, innocently, overseeing the operation.

Teresa's heart went out to Barnie, trapped in the narrow darkness. She couldn't have prevented it, of course. One word out of her, and she'd have been in her own locker, which she didn't begin to fit. So she just pulled her coat out and took her time buttoning it up. Out of the corner of her eye she watched grubby hands twirl Barnie's lock to make sure he was tucked in for the night. She wasn't the only witness. Fifteen, twenty kids saw it all. But who would inform on the Probst Machine and live to tell another tale? There was a lot of nervous chatter, but not a word about lockers. Not even a shriek of approving laughter.

The crowd thinned, shuffling up the aisle past Mrs. DeFalco's desk. A few people slewed their eyes toward Teresa, possibly thinking about informing the teacher that Teresa had committed the crime. It's usually the loner who takes the rap. But the Probst Organization was hanging back, determined to clear the room. So with the Kobra hoods flaring behind them, nobody even looked Mrs. DeFalco's way as they filed out.

In the hall Teresa heard Dolores Schwab whisper to Angela Santorelli, "Of course if it was a Friday night, and the little *troll* had to be in there all *weekend*, I'd be the first one to tell. Like I'm a really caring person, you know?"

Angela nodded, looking sympathetic and proud to know Dolores. Teresa stamped on, keeping ahead of the heavy tread of the Probst Storm Troopers. Then she heard Mrs. DeFalco banging the classroom door shut behind her. No teacher ever lingered long.

Teresa knew the next minute or so required timing and footwork. She moved faster when the rest broke into a run at the sight of the front door. She accelerated, and then veered, bolting down the dark stairs to the basement. Breathing hard, she ran her hand down the tile wall all the way to the lower hall. Even if a Probst spy had been assigned personally to her, she figured this quick diversion would shake him.

It was practically pitch black in the angle under the basement stairs, though not as dark as the inside of a locker. She stood there motionless among cobwebs, listening to the thunder of feet dying away upstairs. She stood there until she heard nothing but distant city sounds and the vibration of the subway deeper in the earth.

She thought about janitors. If Barnie got himself rescued by one of them, she'd be left standing in this evil-smelling basement with no mission. Still this probably wasn't the week for janitors; it rarely was.

Finally she started up the steps. It was vaguely possible that one Probst goon had been left standing guard upstairs. But it was more likely that the whole bunch was out in the school yard, making sure nobody doubled back.

She took a ten-count on each step. At last her head crested the main floor. She scanned the shadowy hallway. By craning her neck, she could see the front door and a wedge of school yard. Out by the fence stood the whole Probst Mafia: Harley surrounded by his Fearful Four in black plastic-leather Windbreakers. Harley wore a real glove-leather white one, with suede piping and snakeskin flaps. They seemed to be satisfied that they were the last ones out, and on a command from Harley they oozed through the gap in the fence and slithered off down the street out of sight.

Teresa set one foot in the direction of homeroom. She treaded lightly, not letting Barnie know rescue was on the way. It might seem more miraculous if she just stepped quietly up and set him free.

She turned the knob on the homeroom door and eased it open. A kid smell lingered in the room under the settling smog of chalk dust. Tan light slivered in around the shades. Teresa made her noiseless way down an aisle, back to the wall of gray and silent lockers.

But it was too silent, she thought suddenly. Barnie couldn't have escaped on his own. Maybe he—her

11

throat began to close up, and her heart hammered. She broke into a sort of gallop.

She hit Barnie's locker at her top speed. The explosive sound of her complete body smacking against the door rippled down the locker row. Even the echo was deafening. But at last Teresa found something to say to Barnie. "Barnie!" she yelled. "Barnie, speak to me!"

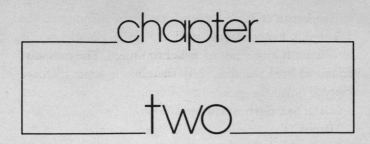

chapter
two

"Chees," said a far-off voice behind the air vents. "What hit me, a truck?"

"Barnie!" Teresa shrieked again, fitting her mouth up to the little slits where her forehead had just connected. "You in there?"

"Where else?" came the far-off voice.

"Help is here!"

"Oh well, yeah. I figured something was," the voice said.

"Just hang in there! I'll have you out in no time."

An answer came from within, but the voice was muffled. "How's that again, Barnie?"

"I said: you won't have me out of this thing until you hear what my combination is. So listen."

"Oh."

"Right to thirty."

Teresa's hands shook, and the little ridges on the combination lock skidded past her fingers. She overshot thirty, whirled the dial, and went for it again. "Okay, thirty."

"Back past thirty to thirteen."

"Right."

"Now up to eighteen."

"Okay."

"What okay?" the locker said. "That's all three numbers. Lift the handle."

Teresa jerked at it, but it wouldn't budge. The air vent sighed.

"Run through those numbers for me one more time," she said, trying for a calm tone. It occurred to her that when she'd banged up against the door, she might have jammed the lock. She had a vision of going for a rescue squad who'd bring an acetylene torch. "What comes after thirty?" she asked, humble now.

"Thirteen. Then eighteen." Was it her imagination, or was his voice getting fainter? Her hand was greasy when she tried to lift the handle a second time. But there was a pleasing sound like a safe being correctly cracked, and Teresa pulled the door open.

Barnie was fitted neatly inside, face forward, with his elbows grazing each wall. He was like a well-preserved find in an Egyptian tomb: King Tut, the Boy Pharaoh, in Levi's. Above and behind him his plaid lumber jacket was still on its hook. Pillowed up against it, his hair fanned out in a halo.

"Chees," Barnie said. "It's—what's your name? Teresa?"

"I just figured I'd come on back and, you know, resc—let you out." Teresa tried to yawn and failed.

"Well, well," Barnie said. "It's a small world. Especially in here."

"You want to come on out?" Teresa wondered why this yo-yo didn't leap out and show a little gratitude.

"My knees seem to be locked," Barnie said. He shook a leg into action and placed a size-four yellow construction boot onto the classroom floor. Looking possibly too calm, he said, "Of course we'll both be back inside if the Kobras are still hanging around. Are they?"

"What do you take me for?" Teresa said. "I waited till they cleared off."

Out of his locker Barnie was a good five inches shorter than she was. "Thanks," he said, looking down at his boots.

"Forget it," she said, hoping he wouldn't.

Teresa waited while he pulled on his jacket; then they walked out of school together. She bent her head down nearer to his, though it added a hump to her back. At the gap in the fence, she said, "You live uptown or downtown?"

"Downtown."

"Me too," said Teresa, who didn't.

"You feel like walking around awhile?" Barnie asked.

"Might as well. I got no plans." This was the truth. They walked past a deli, the Martinizing Dry Cleaners, Ace Hardware, Half-soling While U Wait, a pizza carry-out, Pincus Picture Framers, a Middle-East restaurant, Willoughby's Sash and Door, the Flynn-LaFloria Funeral Establishment. Still nobody said anything. It was dawning on Teresa that rescuing people is easier than making conversation.

She thought of something. Not brilliant, but something. "What was it like in the locker?" Barnie seemed to have forgotten all about the rescue, and she didn't like seeing the whole subject dropped.

"There's not a lot you can do in a situation like that," he said. "It's pretty much breathe in, breathe out."

"Yeah," said Teresa, desperate to make this conversation work, "but—"

"Hold it," Barnie muttered, peering around Teresa's throat down a side street. "What's going on down there?"

A half block away the sidewalk was clogged with a dozen large signs that appeared to be moving on legs. "Let's check this out," he said, cutting around in front of Teresa.

When they got nearer, they saw a bunch of women carrying signs lettered with Magic Markers:

This Site Unsafe
For Our Children

and

BULLDOZE OR
TANGLE WITH US

and

Mothers' March
For A
Half-Decent City

They were picketing in front of a high wooden construction fence. Above it a building was sagging out at a sharp angle toward the sidewalk.

The building must have been three or four stories tall at one time. But its top looked now like it had been eaten by prehistoric beasts. The windows were gone, and the sills were charred. "See these kids?" a woman yelled, stepping out of the picket line and pointing a sign at Teresa and Barnie. It read:

WORRIED MOMS
ARE TAXPAYERS TOO

Teresa and Barnie ducked behind a parked DeVille ragtop, but the woman kept poking her sign at them over the car hood. "Kids like these," she roared, "can't even play on the sidewalks of this so-called city without getting some wall down on their heads! What they going to do without safe streets where we can keep an eye on them? I'll tell you what! Smoke dope under bushes! You want me to tell you what else they'll do?"

Just then a Ford Econoline van with eyes painted on it came down the middle of the street. "Television news!" the women all shrieked and broke ranks. "Network coverage," they hollered. "Maybe live!" They pounded off to meet the van, which disappeared behind their signs.

Teresa stood with one elbow on the DeVille's fender. Looking up at the building, she had to agree that its days were numbered. She turned to make this remark to Barnie. But he was gone.

He wasn't the type to go flying off to get his face on the *Six O'Clock News* or even *Good Morning, America.* Teresa figured maybe he'd just cut out, like people often did. "Wouldn't be the first time," she said, probably to herself, slapping her hand down on the fender.

"Hey, Teresa, don't. You'll scare it." It was Barnie's voice, muffled like in the locker.

Now where's that little devil got to? Teresa wondered. She checked around on the curb side of the DeVille. There was Barnie squatting down by a parking meter.

He was eye to eye with the sorriest-looking street cat Teresa ever saw. Barnie's hand was out, and the cat was interested. It stood on three legs with a front paw drawn up, undecided. Its nose twitched little nerve-racked questions. One ear was standing tall. The other one was missing.

After a moment more of hesitation the cat decided Barnie was probably a poor risk. It drew back, but it didn't take its eyes off him. Another starving cat, Teresa thought. Its ribs were sticking out so far it looked like a fur birdcage, which in a way it probably was. Then the cat turned tail and darted through a missing board in the fence.

"It's probably got distemper," Teresa started to say, but something sad and serious in Barnie's face stopped her. He mumbled something.

"Say what?"

"I said there's a lot of misery in this city. It's a rough life, on all levels."

Teresa was prepared to give this some thought, but a more pressing matter suddenly arose. "Barnie." She nudged him with her toe.

"I guess I'll go on home," Barnie mumbled.

"You'll never make it," Teresa said, urgent now. "Take a look back at the corner." Down by the Flynn-LaFloria Funeral Establishment a black and white blob had formed. It was no funeral, except maybe theirs. It was a nest of Kobras.

Teresa saw the flash of Harley Probst's Windbreaker. They'd all probably spot Teresa—and worse yet, Barnie —in a matter of seconds.

19

In the other direction the street was blocked by worried moms and the TV van. There was a camera on the van roof now, panning across the jiggling signs.

Teresa and Barnie moved at the same time, through the opening in the fence, and then did a kind of wild dance over heaps of bricks and garbage. There was only a narrow space between the fence and the building. The front stoop was gone, and the charred doorsill was on a level with Teresa's shoulders, which put it nearly over Barnie's head.

"We can't hang out around here," she said. "If the Kobras saw us, they'll be through that fence like a SWAT team. Probably come in here snooping around anyway."

"Let's get into the building," Barnie said, looking up at the front doorway.

Teresa wondered how he figured he could leap higher than his head to get there. But she sensed the Kobras sliding closer.

So she laced her fingers and made a foothold. Barnie placed a construction boot on it and sprang up into the doorway. He seemed to take flight, and she saw him land like a parachutist in reverse. His head reappeared very low, just above the charred sill. "I think they're heading this way."

He dropped down his arms. Teresa grabbed his wrists and tried to walk up the wall. "Hold it!" Barnie gasped. "You're no human fly, Teresa. And you're going to pull my hands off."

Grabbing an old crate, Teresa set it down and jumped from it, nearly making it onto the doorsill. Her legs fanned the air. Barnie managed to yank her all the way in, scooping off the bottom three buttons on her coat. They both lay heaped in an old hallway filled with piles of plaster and bent six-penny nails.

Lightly toasted laths hung out of the see-through walls. A dead light fixture swung from a frayed cord. "The worried moms weren't wrong," Teresa said. "This place is a real health hazard."

"So are the Kobras," Barnie said. "We better get away from the front door. The TV camera may try for a shot of this place."

They crept back through the hallway. A bald carpet running down the center sagged severely in the middle of the hall. "Probably a hole under that," Barnie pointed out. "Hug the wall."

Curling wallpaper with blue roses kept brushing Teresa's ear. She thought of spiders but said nothing. When Barnie started up a stairway with a missing banister, she wondered about the floor above.

He seemed to read her thoughts. Halfway to the landing he said over his shoulder, "Look, if we fall through the floor upstairs, we'll be back where we started. If we fall through the floor here, we'll be in the cellar."

Picturing a pit full of brown things with teeth, swimming in slime, Teresa wondered what would stop them from falling through both floors. But on she went. They filed up the chattering stairs in a storm of dust and a

21

riot of reaches. And Teresa followed Barnie, though she wasn't used to following anybody. Or having anybody to follow.

Outside Harley Probst and his Kobras were drawing nearer the TV van, on the lookout for a little action.

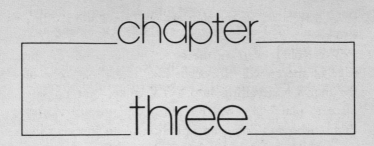

chapter

three

Upstairs it was brighter. A breeze blew straight through empty windows in the front to the missing back wall. It even smelled somewhat better up there. The floor looked reasonably safe. There were high stacks of brown-edged newspapers, a clutch of dusty Thunderbird bottles, and a hypodermic needle; but nothing looked too recent.

Barnie kept close to the wall and worked his way toward the front of the house. Directly over the front door was a long window covered on the inside with shutters. By looking through the slits between the slats, Teresa and Barnie had a view of the street.

The TV van was directly in front of them now. The roof camera moved back and forth between the worried moms and the building. The camera's eye occasionally panned right across the shutters on Teresa and Barnie's window.

The Kobras were in the street, hanging out on the edge of the crowd. "Innocent kids like these," one of the moms was yelling into a TV mike, "got no safe place to play." She was poking a sign toward Harley Probst who was doing an imitation of an innocent kid at play. He tried to skip a little, but he was rusty. "That building could come down any minute!" the mom yelled.

One of the Kobras eased around to the back of the TV van where nobody was. He started to work down low, prying off a hubcap.

"I wish they'd all clear out—especially that Probst bunch—before this building really does cave in," Teresa whispered.

Barnie nodded. "We're trapped up here till they do. It's no different from being back in the locker."

Not quite, Teresa thought. At least here it's the two of us. She really wanted to say that when a haze of dust from the shutters made her sneeze. It wasn't loud, but she jerked, ramming her elbow into the shutter on her side. It popped off its hinges and started to fall out in slow motion.

"Look at that! See what we mean?" one of the moms yelled while the shutter was still in the air. Teresa jumped back out of sight. But Barnie never left his post. The two of them watched the shutter balance on the fence and then tip over on the street side.

It hit not far from Harley's boot. He stepped back behind one of his Kobras. Teresa knew it was a Kobra rule that in times of danger they were supposed to protect their leader.

The falling shutter seemed to be the last straw for the TV people. Any minute now the entire building could be in the street with the van underneath. It jerked into low gear, and the moms followed, still brandishing their signs. Only Harley Probst's Kobras were left on the empty street.

"In about a minute," Barnie said, "the Kobras will start exploring around here."

"Then we've had it," Teresa said. "If we go, we'll go together, Barnie."

"Look for something heavy," he replied. "Anything heavy and hurry up." Barnie squinted through the shutter on his side. He looked like a sentry up on a fortress wall. He didn't even look short, Teresa noticed.

In the first room she came to, all the plaster was on the floor. She worked a loose brick out of the wall and darted back across the groaning floor.

"Step on it," Barnie murmured from the window. "They've figured out how to get through the fence." By then he'd quietly folded back the shutter on his side. He and Teresa crouched by the sill.

Directly below, the Kobras were assembling under the front door. They were discussing in their usual grunts the best way to get up into the building. "Be a good clubhouse," Harley growled.

25

And the rest of them said, "Yeah, Harley." "Great plan, Harley." "Leave it to you to think of a really good idea, Harley."

"Shut up," Harley said.

He sent all four Kobras up into the building to check the place out. Harley was taking no chances on falling through a weak floor. Teresa and Barnie heard the Kobras grunting and rummaging beneath their feet.

She noticed that Barnie's hand was only resting lightly on the brick and began to have a truly foreboding feeling. "Maybe if there's a closet around here somewhere, we could . . ." Then she remembered Barnie's being in the locker. Too much of that kind of thing in one day could be—too much of that kind of thing.

She was eyeing the top of the stairs, waiting to see heads, when the Kobras started thrashing around, still directly underneath. "Hey, Harley! Looks like we got company in here!"

Teresa's blood froze. Then there was a scream, not hers. It came from downstairs. "The cat," Barnie whispered, peering straight down at the top of Harley's head. "They threw the cat out, and Harley's got it."

Teresa chanced a quick look. Harley was holding the one-eared cat by the tail. It was twisting in the air, and its claws were out. It was doing its best to throw cat punches at Harley. But he held it well away from his white Windbreaker.

"A cat's what we don't need in a clubhouse," he said.

"You can say that again," the Kobras chorused.

"I say something one time, you remember it," Harley

26

snarled. He started swinging the cat then. It knew it was in real trouble. Its paws curled in, and its one ear folded flat. "You guys are about to see one cat splattered all over that fence."

"Haul off and let her fly," one of the Kobras said.

Teresa and Barnie could hear the cat's hopeless hissing from where they crouched. Harley was swinging it higher and higher. The tip of its tail tried to curl around his fist. Then it was only a circular screaming blur in the air.

Quicker than Teresa saw, Barnie snatched up the brick. There was nothing to it. He didn't even aim. The brick dropped like a lesson in gravity. It hit Harley's skull squarely. Then the brick slid down the back of his Windbreaker as Harley slipped to the ground. He settled in the shape of the letter *S*.

Somehow, with the suddenness of it all, Harley didn't let go of the cat's tail until he hit the ground. It landed on his face, all its claws digging in. Then it was on top of the brick pile, traveling. Then it was gone.

"Uhhhh," one of the Kobras said from the doorway. "You guys see that? Say, listen, Harley, you hurt?" No answer. The Kobras shifted their feet.

Finally another Kobra asked, "If he's dead, who gets the Windbreaker?"

27

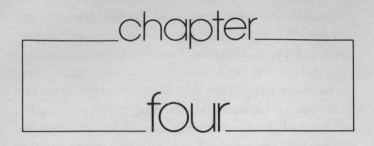

chapter

four

Teresa couldn't take her eyes off Harley, sprawled there
with the rest of the garbage. She'd have been just as
happy if he moved or something. The Kobras sounded
like they were colliding with each other in the downstairs hall. The whole building trembled. The place
could collapse before they'd be able to come to a decision
without their leader. The cat scratches were showing
up on Harley's face. His eyes stayed shut.

Barnie was staring down too. Teresa didn't know
where to begin with him. She wanted to say: this'll
teach Harley to mess with cats. And: listen, if you've
killed him and have to do time, count on me to wait,
years even. But mainly she wanted to say: maybe the
Kobras will just think it was a loose brick since they
still don't know we're up here.

Before she could open her mouth, Harley's arm moved. His right hand jerked around by itself, trying to find his head. He pulled himself up on his left elbow and rubbed the hand through his hair. Then he examined his fingers. They were dripping red. His face crumpled. He began to bawl softly.

At that the Kobras bailed out of the building and stood in a circle around him. His sobs merged into a series of loud hiccups. "Hey, Harley," said a Kobra, shuffling his boots. "Whatcha wanna do that for?"

"Shut up," Harley whimpered. He explored the top of his head again, flinching. Then he made the mistake of wiping his hands on his Windbreaker.

It was streaked red and white like a barber pole. The Kobras couldn't take their eyes off it. Harley had always kept it so white. Without a spotless real leather Windbreaker Harley was losing points. He almost didn't seem like a leader anymore. The crying was clearly another strike against him, though he was drying up now.

Teresa sat back on her heels, reasonably pleased with the scene below. Harley had just had the first disciplining of his life. She knew that in a little while, when he'd pulled himself together, the Kobras would all wander off. It was a bad-luck-type place for them.

But then she noticed Barnie was still hanging his head far out the window. When Harley's eyes focused, he could look straight up and spot Barnie. The next thing was incredible. Teresa clutched her forehead—Barnie was yelling down at them!

"Hey, Harley, and you other wimps!"

29

The Kobras jumped at this voice from heaven.

"I got a pile of bricks up here, one for each head. Yeah, I got another one for you too, Harley!"

This tough, suicidal talk coming out of Barnie's mouth nearly blew Teresa away. She didn't see any pile of bricks handy either. He's got to be out of his gourd, she thought desperately. We'd have been home free if he'd kept his yap shut. There's such a thing as too much guts.

"The next time you feel like snuffing a cat, remember how it feels to have a brick dropped on your soft head!" Barnie wouldn't quit.

The red eyes in Harley's lolling head focused on Barnie. Barnie, who was scheduled to be spending the night in his own locker. Harley's eyes seem to expand and contract at the same time. Teresa withered. So did the Kobras. A sudden rain of bricks could fall any old time now.

The moment seemed to linger to eternity. And in it Teresa made a decision she wouldn't be able to reverse. She swallowed once and stuck her head out the window, next to Barnie's.

They saw her, all of them. Harley, his Kobras. Their lips were curling, but their eyes were haunted. And they were assuming various tough poses, but nothing convincing. Then, with bricks still clearly on their minds, the Kobras broke ranks and scattered, heads low. There was a bottleneck at the opening in the fence when all four of them tried to get through it at once. Then a minor tie-up when they tried it two by two. Finally they discovered single file, casting cautious glances at the window where Teresa's head still appeared next to Barnie's. She wished she had a brick herself.

Below her, alone in a pile of chicken bones and exhausted spray cans with a lump rising on his head and the blood settling into his Windbreaker, Harley tried to think. Teresa could see it wasn't easy for him. Nobody had ever dared lay a finger on him, much less a brick.

He struggled up on one knee, never taking his eyes off Barnie. "Say, listen, Barn. You were right about those guys, callin' 'em wimps and like that. You see them yellowbellies light out when they thought you had some more bricks up there? You ain't got any more bricks up there, do you . . . buddy?"

"I got a pile of them," Barnie called down.

"Twenty at least," Teresa put in. "No, let's see. Twenty-three, twenty-four. And all ready to haul off and let fly."

"Say listen, Barnie," Harley continued, "how'd you like to join the King Kobras? I mean we could use a few good men like you."

"Could you use a few good women too?" Teresa called down.

"Yuch!" Harley retched without thinking.

Teresa muttered to Barnie, "He's not only a Kobra, he's a pig."

"I don't know, Harley," Barnie yelled down. "I don't think I'd want the responsibility of leading a gang. Even a nothing outfit like the Puff Adders or whatever you call yourselves."

"Leading?" Harvey croaked. "Leading? Who said anything about leading? *I'm* the leader!" He fingered his Windbreaker. "You kidding? Whatsamatta with you?" This was too much. He started scuttling crab-wise across the garbage, making for the fence. "You lead the Kobras? The Kobras bein' run by a *dwarf?*"

"Well, I don't know," Barnie said to the scuttling figure. "They may be looking for leadership right now." He stared off down the street. "Wherever they are."

Tears glistened in Harley's eyes, tears of pure rage. He clutched his head which seemed to be pounding.

"Okay, Barnie," he said, "you've blown it. Nobody leans on Harley Probst. I been good to you, but now you've had it—and so's that dizzy chick—what's her name—Teresa. Next time I see either one of you, I'll squash you like bugs. Do yourselves a favor and vanish because next time . . ."

Harley stood up by the missing board in the fence and ran a red finger across his throat. Then he was through the fence and sprinting down the sidewalk. He skidded to a stop when he was well out of range. "I mean this," he yelled back, almost sadly. "You die."

Teresa dropped to the floor and crumpled. "He'll have those Kobras on a short leash before night. They can't function without him."

"I guess we were sort of a blow to his pride," Barnie said.

"I got to hand it to you, Barnie. You hung really tough."

"So did you, Teresa."

"So what do we do for an encore?" she said. "Go through the rest of our lives with a ladder and a handful of bricks and try to keep directly over Harley's head? It isn't practical."

"He won't rest till he's got us," Barnie said. "And we're outnumbered. Tomorrow at school—"

"Don't mention school," Teresa said. "We'd never make it to lunchtime." They sat there watching the shadows stretch longer on the floor. There was only the distant boom of evening rush-hour traffic. "I guess we'll have to go away somewheres, Barn."

"You mean—run away? Where?"

"Do I know? Anyplace. Where do runaways go? You hear about them all the time on TV. *Sixty Minutes* even."

"Yeah, but don't they end up in night court or mugged or like that?" Barnie said.

"Maybe only the ones who run away on their own." Teresa examined the brick dust on her hand and slanted a look at Barnie. "You know—loners. Not like us."

"What about your family, Teresa? What would they think?"

"What they?" Teresa replied. "There's only one, and she's part-time. My aunt. She hasn't been home since Thursday. She's in and out, mostly out. I figure I could graduate high school, get married, have a couple kids and maybe a career on the side before she noticed."

Teresa thought that about covered her family background. But no. Something weird and unfamiliar came over her. Nobody had ever asked her even that much about who she was, where she came from. Nobody but Barnie.

A lump formed in her throat, but she felt like talking around it. Right here in this wrecked building or house or whatever, she realized she had something to remember.

"I had family once," she told Barnie. "Not so much parents; they're pretty much of a blur. But I had a grandmother."

She paused then, to remember more—and to see if he was still interested. He seemed to be.

"I don't remember that much about her. She was pretty nice, I guess. She lived—way out someplace. My aunt and I, we took a subway and then a bus. My grandmother had a garden. Sort of one, with beans that grew up the fence and tomato plants tied up on sticks. She probably never had to defrost anything to eat. But what I really remember was her sitting on the back steps snapping beans into a pan and watching me run up and down her garden rows. I was the same size as the tomato stakes. She was pretty nice, I think . . ."

Teresa blinked and returned to the present. Barnie was sitting beside her with the soles of his boots together and his small knees stuck out. He was fiddling with some bottle caps on the floor, but he'd heard her. He was a good listener. She cleared her throat.

"I'll send her a card when we get there. My aunt, I mean."

"Get where?"

"Wherever. You got a family, Barnie?"

"Foster family."

"Like you're adopted?"

"Naw. I never was too adoptable. I started out in an incubator in an orphanage. I was premature, a preemie. Not that I remember it, but I saw my records once, after I could read. The way I figure it, nobody wanted to adopt me, and then I was too old. So I got put in with a foster family. The government pays them to keep me."

Teresa compared her grandmother to an incubator, and her eyes began to sting. She pulled herself together. "The government pays them?"

Barnie nodded and made a kind of chess move with a bottle cap.

"So the government stops paying them if you're not there?"

He nodded again. "They'll keep getting the checks as long as they don't report me missing."

"Call that case closed," Teresa said. "So what's stopping us?"

"Money," Barnie said. He jammed his hands into his lumber-jacket pocket. His eyes lighted cautiously. "Mrs. DeFalco forgot to collect our bus-pass money today." He pulled out two rumpled singles.

Teresa ran a finger around the inside of her left sock, where she banked. Even muggers don't check your socks unless they're kinky. "You know, you're right." She drew out a pair of bills. "How far do you think this'll take us?"

"Out of town," Barnie said.

"Far enough away from Harley and the Kobras?"

"The Bermuda Triangle wouldn't be far enough for that," he answered. "Still, if you're going to run away, you got to take that first step."

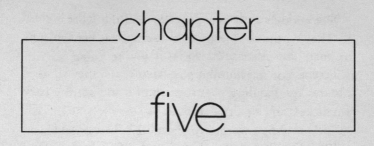

chapter

five

They made it on foot to the bus station, safe in the undertow of the homeward-bound commuters.

Out on the platforms where the buses were gunning, carbon monoxide turned the evening blue around them. "This could kill you quicker than Harley," Barnie said. He elbowed into a line for a bus full of standees. "What's a two-dollar stop on this route?" Teresa heard him yell up into the bus.

"A dumb question," the driver replied.

By now Teresa had pushed up past a line of briefcases. She even edged Barnie out of the way. Fixing an eye on the driver, who was clearly on a short fuse, she said, "Let's try that again. How far will a couple bucks take you?"

The heel of the driver's hand was banging the bottom of the steering wheel. He wouldn't look at her but said, "A buck ninety-five takes you to Paradise Park."

Teresa turned a thumb-up at Barnie, and they climbed into the bus, handing over four singles and getting back two nickels and a pair of stubs.

"Tell us when we get to Paradise," Teresa said.

"Paradise Park," the driver said. "Get back behind the white line."

After a couple of stops in the near-in suburbs the bus cleared out, and Barnie and Teresa could find seats. It was nearly dark when the bus made a stop at a place called Oradell. There were lights on in the houses, throwing yellow shapes out across the lawns. Swings, slides, above-ground pools stood like lonely sculpture.

Inside kitchens families were sitting around dinette sets, eating their heads off. Teresa's stomach, queasy all morning and knotted all afternoon, unfurled. There was an answering sigh from under Barnie's belt buckle. But they said nothing. The bus gunned on, past a McDonald's and a Dunkin' Donuts side by side. Teresa and Barnie sat staring into their dark laps.

"What could we get for a nickel apiece?" Barnie muttered.

"Ball gum out of a machine if we're lucky." But Teresa wasn't that hungry yet. She was thinking about Paradise Park.

She pictured this wonderful place with tall open iron gates and little gravel walks between flower beds without litter. And arching bridges over ponds. No—there'd be streams or brooks where you could wash your face. You'd dip your hand down, and the water would be alive with goldfish. And there'd be swans, luminous in the evening. And maybe a bandstand strung with colored lights. And a small combo with Shaun Cassidy softly singing, "Do You Believe in Magic?" to nobody but her and Barnie. Squirrels, not rats. Swans, not pigeons. Frogs, not Kobras.

A lot of flowers, all kinds. Maybe even tomato plants on stakes and beans running up fences—anything you wanted. And they'd close the wrought-iron gates at night, and you'd sleep on moss, safer than you'd ever been.

In her mind she was already there. When the monster trailer trucks rocketed past the bus, setting up a vacuum, she heard only the little woodland night sounds of Paradise Park: Shaun Cassidy and nesting doves.

Barnie's head was down, but his eyes seemed to be open. "What do you think it'll be like?" she asked him.

"Paradise Park? The way I figure it," Barnie said, "it's probably one of those retirement communities they advertise in the Sunday paper."

Teresa could visualize Barnie reading the Sunday paper, every section, every Sunday. Even classified.

"They give them names like that," he said. "Paradise Park. Sunset Acres. Maturity Manor. Last Roundup Village. They pay people to think up the names."

"How in the devil are we going to fit into an old

39

folks' town?" Teresa asked, her dream beginning to disintegrate.

"It could work out," Barnie said. "We might be kind of . . ."

"Kind of grandchildren for them?"

"Maybe," he said, shrugging a little. "Maybe."

The bus swung off the highway, and the doors folded open. "End of the line," the driver said, flipping money out of the cashbox. "Paradise Park."

Teresa and Barnie stepped down onto blacktop. The bus made an arc, shot a final death ray of exhaust at them, and heaved back onto the highway, back to the city.

In front of them black pavement stretched forever—to Alaska. They were standing on the outer arrows of a parking lot. If Shaun Cassidy was anywhere around, he was buried six feet under asphalt. Teresa felt the rest of her dream crumble.

In the distance past a clutter of parked cars, she could make out a vast jumble of steel, glass, and white brick. In letters of fire a neon sign read:

PARADISE PARK

"Shoot," Barnie said. "It's a shopping mall."

They looked at each other. But there was no going

back now, not with a dime between them and Harley Probst in their past.

"Fur's beginning to form on my teeth," Barnie said.

"Fur's what?"

"It's beginning to form on my teeth. It does that whenever it's night and I know I'm not going to be able to brush. My teeth."

Teresa considered this. You probably shouldn't laugh off other people's problems when they're willing to share them. "That's a worry," she said. "I can relate to that. But it may not be our Number One problem."

All their problems were nearly solved when a blind-eyed Mazda station wagon plunged across the lot against the arrow. They jumped apart just as the brights flicked on, and the Mazda shot between them. It gunned along inches from smearing Teresa and Barnie all over the lot.

At the wheel was a woman driving one-handed with a baby in a car seat and a hatchback full of deck furniture.

"What are ya, crazy?" Teresa howled into the tail-lights. When they came back together, Teresa took Barnie's hand, which was already reaching for hers.

They moved nearer the main doors of the mall under a sign reading: OPEN TILL NINE THIRTY NIGHTLY. Automatic doors opened to receive them and whisked shut behind them, closing out the world.

More shoppers were leaving than arriving, but there was still enough of a crowd to get comfortably lost in. A small kid was being dragged through the doors by a

41

father in a large T-shirt that read, "I'd Rather Be Surfing." The kid was hanging onto a cone of frozen yogurt and trying to get loose from his father. A blob of the yogurt splatted onto the floor. Teresa and Barnie watched it spread over the tile.

Paradise Park was brighter than a city street and totally climate controlled. Palm trees and regular trees grew in long planters down the center in front of hundreds of shops without doors. There was even a creek, more or less, full of plastic water lilies and pennies. Small arching bridges crossed it every few yards. No swans, Teresa noted, but still—

"Nobody's going to find us here," Barnie muttered. They'd fallen into a line of moving shoppers.

"Like who?"

"Like anybody. Harley Probst and the Kobras. Attendance officers from schools. Cops even. Harley Probst. Whoever."

Teresa plodded at his side, hunching a little, but less. She held her breath past a place called Karmelkorn Kastle. Exhaling against the scent of sweet syrup, she read the sign on the corn popper: LARGE BAGS 80¢. SUPER SIZE 95¢. BELLY-BUSTERS $1.25. The nickel in her pocket seemed to turn over by itself in embarrassment. She felt her coat with the scooped-off buttons grow bigger over her shrinking frame.

On they moved down an endless, glittering vista of palm trees and caramel corn, of neon and MASTER CHARGE ACCEPTED, of SE HABLA ESPAÑOL and GIFT WRAPPING AT NO ADDITIONAL CHARGE.

"It's bigger than the city," Barnie said. They were shuffling past a stereo store called Audio Jungle. And then past The Tennis Connection. And Shirt Tales. And Milady Maternity Modes. Past a place with a sign reading, CANDLES IN SHAPES YOU NEVER THOUGHT OF.

"And a lot cleaner," Teresa said. It was possible to keep up her spirits as long as these stores stayed open, as long as it wasn't nine thirty, closing hour. Live for the moment, Teresa thought, and stopped breathing again past a provolone-and-liverwurst-smelling place called The Barnyard Connoisseur.

Barnie stepped out of the line of shuffling shoppers and gathered up a wadded shopping bag wedged under the lip of the creek. "Everybody's got one," he said, smoothing it out. "It'll help us look right."

Teresa read the bag: "Milady Maternity Modes." They were near the end of the creek. It terminated in an aluminum-sided wishing well. She veered over, fumbled the nickel out of her pocket, and flipped it into the well. "What did you do that for?" Barnie asked.

"For luck, what else? We'll need it."

"You got something there." Barnie fished up his nickel and let it fly.

They watched the coin turn in the air, and they watched the wishing well swallow it. Above them, across the end of the mall, was a giant sign above the doors to a department store. FORBES & LEDSMAR it said in dramatic, back-lit letters.

"What do you think?" Barnie ran a finger under his nose. "In or out?"

"We better keep moving without doubling back," Teresa said.

They moved forward into the entryway of the store where a blast of French perfume cut at their eyes. Blinking, Barnie pulled Teresa over by a sand-filled chrome ashtray. A sign over it in curling letters read:

*Smoking is a no-no
in Forbes & Ledsmar.
Be a darling and cooperate.*

"This place looks pretty fancy-schmancy," Barnie muttered. "Maybe we better . . ." His face went blank. Still intelligent, but blank.

"Better what?" Teresa said. "We better not be out in that main hall when they shut down for the night. What are we going to do, sleep in the maternity shopping bag?"

Barnie looked shaken. "I guess we could go out and find a car to sleep in."

"You kidding? Who leaves a car here overnight, locked or not? By nine forty that parking lot's going to look like the Gobi Desert. We'd be sitting ducks. It may even be raining. Who can tell in here?"

A last-minute shopper barreled in behind them, elbowed Teresa aside to jam a cigarette into the ashtray, and absentmindedly slammed Barnie into an inner door which opened automatically. He was spilled suddenly into the store and fell to his knees in lipstick-pink carpeting where he seemed to sink.

The shopping bag skidded across pink pile and was shredded beneath the feet of departing shoppers.

Teresa grabbed him under one arm and raised him to his feet. "Act normal," she whispered, wondering how.

They were at the edge of the Costume Jewelry section. The rest of the store stretched to infinity, bigger than Gimbels. A shadow fell across them. Teresa looked up at an astonishing figure—a tall young woman carrying a velvet tray. She seemed to be a page ripped out of *Vogue* magazine. And her entire head appeared to have been applied by a tiny brush. The model looked down at Teresa in more ways than one. "Free sample, sweetie?"

"Something to eat?" Teresa was hopeful.

"Perfume, dearest."

"No thanks."

Barnie nudged her. "Better take it. You don't know where your next bath's coming from."

Teresa stuck out her hand and palmed a bottle the size of a bullet into her pocket. They walked on until the escalators were in sight. The clock overhead stood at nine fifteen. The Down escalator was full; the Up was empty. Teresa and Barnie started up.

They could almost read each other without words, Teresa thought. It looked good too, like they weren't plotting. They knew where they were going. They were even managing to time it right. They just didn't know how they were going to pull it off once they got there.

45

The seventh-floor clock said twenty-five past when they found the department they'd been looking for. Coolly Teresa and Barnie walked under the big sign that read:

BEDS & BEDDING

Another five minutes and the gong sounded throughout the store, signaling the end of the shopping day.

chapter

six

It was midnight—at least. The store had been silent for hours, maybe eons. There'd been nothing to hear since the distant sound of push brooms soon after nine thirty.

At least nothing Teresa could hear from under a queen-size bed in Beds & Bedding on the seventh floor. She was lying blind, and for all she knew, deaf. Lightly cradled in dust on vinyl, she was screened on four sides by a candlewick bedspread.

She hadn't meant to sleep a wink, but she must have because she'd been dreaming. A real horror show of a dream. In it she'd been buried in a coffin which was actually a school locker laid flat. She'd even watched herself being lowered into a creepy grave. Then at the end of the dream, grubby hands had worked the combination and thrown the locker door open. The sunshine streamed in, and Harley Probst drove a stake through her heart.

After that, she woke up and found herself under a bed but still half in the dream. It took her a minute to realize that she was not only under a bed but in a closed department store in the middle of the night. She worked a hand out across inky blackness. Barnie wasn't there.

She stifled a gasp and made herself remember. Just as the store closed, they'd dived for cover, splitting up without thinking. When the coast was clear of clerks, Teresa had dropped down beside a queen-size with a long drooping cover on it and rolled under.

At the same time she had a vague impression of Barnie falling onto another bed across the aisle. It was a weird, heart-shaped bed, king-size at least, covered in quilted black satin. Then the lights went out, and none of the footsteps in the Beds & Bedding department came nearer.

Something—someone was coming nearer now, though. And it wasn't Barnie. Teresa froze. She inhaled dust and stared sightless at black innersprings. Footsteps seemed to be coming from the escalator, unless she'd got her directions mixed up. A heavy tread in soft-soled shoes. Grunts too—hardly human. Now wavering light filtered through the bedspread: possibly a flashlight being beamed down the aisles.

"Awright, giddouta there," a voice boomed, practically on top of her.

Teresa stopped breathing.

48

The bedspread twitched just beside her right shoulder. A head poked under the spread, lifting it in a pale pyramid of light. Teresa's mouth opened, but nothing came out. The head wasn't human. Yellow eyes, glowing. Teeth. Fur standing out all around like a halo. It was a cat.

"I said giddouta there, Pantyhose," the voice boomed from above again. The cat looked astonished to find Teresa under the bed. But someone grabbed the cat's tail. The cat face vanished suddenly with the sound of claws skidding across vinyl tile. The bedspread fell back into place, but not before Teresa saw a pair of big carpet slippers splayed out below two pants legs thick as trees.

Whoever it was seemed to have his hands full with a cat and a flashlight. Beams of light seemed to be dancing all over the dark department. "You little faker," the voice boomed. "How am I gonna make my rounds with you pokin' your snout under every bed. Whattsamatta with you anyways?"

Nightwatchman, Teresa thought numbly . . . and a watch*cat*?

"Scratch me, willya? Why, I oughta . . ."

The cat hit the floor on all four paws. It burrowed beneath the candlewick spread again and was immediately all over Teresa. Somehow it twitched itself between her face and the innersprings, crouching there and sniffing around like mad. Teresa felt claws and lay lifeless.

She heard the nightwatchman grunt again, as if he

49

were about to go down on one knee and shine the light under the bed. A knee joint creaked.

". . . Aw forget it. Giddouta my life if that's the way you're gonna act. You catch me chasin' a retarded cat all over Beds and Bedding? Forget it. Go on back to Hosiery. I got *The Late Show* to watch upstairs in TV and Sound Systems."

The carpet slippers shambled away, farther off. The cat stirred and walked the length of Teresa, nipping her ankle in passing. Then it exited through the spread at the foot of the bed. Teresa swallowed dryly, fear and fur all over her face. Dark silence descended again.

An age passed before she heard another voice. "Teresa?" It was a whisper, but it carried all over the silent, waiting floor. It was Barnie.

Teresa lifted the bedspread hem and rolled out into the aisle. "Will he come back, do you think?" she whispered to the ceiling.

The heart-shaped black bed beside her seemed to speak: "Sounds like he's one floor up watching TV," Barnie said, which was no answer. With a slick sound he slid over satin. His construction boots came into view directly above Teresa. Then his head. He looked down and said, "We probably shouldn't even talk."

"You kidding?" she said. "A person could go crazy."

"Don't I know?" Barnie whispered over her. "It wasn't more than eight hours or so since the Kobras put me in the locker. I'll show you crazy if this keeps up."

"I know," Teresa said. "It's been one of those days."

"You want to get back under the bed?" Barnie said. "Because I'm getting to the point where I actually need small places."

They slipped in under the queen-size and settled down there, shoulder to shoulder. It seemed to make them the same size. "This place is filthy under here," Teresa said. "The dust is phenomenal. Don't they ever sweep out?"

"You better be glad they didn't tonight."

"I know, but trying not to sneeze is taking up too much of my concentration. I tried not to sleep too, but I did, a little. Did you?"

"On that heart-shaped bed, you kidding? I got the pillows out from under that black cover thing and poked them down behind the headboard. Then I climbed in under the cover and tried to be the same shape as the pillows. But I couldn't get comfortable along the top of the heart shape. It caught me right in the back. I must've panicked to think I could pass myself off as a couple of pillows. How'd you manage?"

"Okay, except when that cockamamie cat came under here and walked all over my head. What's her name— *Pantyhose?* Whatever, she's got a set of claws on her that won't stop. For a minute I thought she was a rat, but then I realized the nightwatchman was talking to her. Or somebody. Was he alone?"

"Did I ask him?" Barnie said. "Can a pillow sit up and look around? I got the cat too. She sat right on my face, and she weighs a ton. We've had cats all day. I used to like them."

51

"Well, at least she's not going to tell on us. But do you think they'll make another round tonight?"

Barnie was thinking—Teresa could almost feel him weighing the situation, playing the odds.

"The way I see it is this," Barnie whispered finally. "Coming up to Beds and Bedding was a natural reaction. It's our first night. We're being forced into a lot of quick decisions. So we make a beeline to beds, without thinking through that we can't sleep on them, since we'd be out there in the open. Still this wasn't a bad place because at least we can get out of sight, though I'm swearing off that heart-shaped thing."

"True," Teresa muttered. "I mean where would we go in the Bath Shop for instance—into a soap dish?"

"Right. So even if we can't get comfortable, this wasn't the worst choice for a couple of tyros."

"Couple of what?"

"Tyros," Barnie said. "You know—beginners."

"Barnie, you got a vocabulary on you like I cannot believe."

"Vocabulary won't save us," he said. "Planning will. A couple of cool heads is what we need. Thinking every minute, calculating every move."

"Suits me," Teresa said. "And since we're at the end of the bus line, illegally on the seventh floor of a closed department store, buried alive under a bed, dead broke, and certain to face a messy death if we ever turn up in Kobra territory again . . . I mean when you consider the situation, it calls for cool heads."

52

Barnie nodded. Teresa heard his head give the floor little pats.

"On the plus side," she added, "there'll be no school for us tomorrow."

"True," Barnie said. "But let's not get shortsighted. School's strictly a thing of the past for us."

"Yeah?" Teresa said, turning to see if she could make out the small, firm-chinned outline of Barnie's profile. "How long we going to be here?"

"Well, look at it this way. A big store like this is a total life-support system, right? I figure we can settle in for quite awhile, if we don't get caught."

"Like for how long?"

"Quite awhile," Barnie said. "Till we're grown."

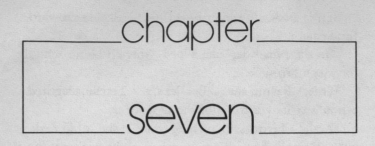

chapter

seven

"One footstep could give us away," Barnie said. "What can you see?"

They'd taken off their shoes and lined them up under Teresa's bed. The enormous dark store waited all around them.

"I can see more and more," Teresa answered, "like a bat. Looks like somebody left a bedside lamp on over there somewhere."

"Then we keep away from it. We got to fight our instincts and move away from light sources, not toward. And let's try not to run into each other too much."

"I guess as long as we can hear that TV going up there—"

"I got no faith in that TV set. He could leave it on

while he makes a second sweep. Let's work over toward the escalator."

"Up or Down?"

"Both," Barnie said.

"You don't mean we split up?" Teresa clutched Barnie's sleeve.

"No. First up, then down. Together."

They took the escalator a step at a time, Teresa on Barnie's heels. She only chanced a look out over the store when they were nearly up to eight. The little nozzles on the sprinkler system all over the seventh-floor ceiling stretched away into the gloom. Feeling a little dizzy, Teresa climbed on, right up Barnie's heels.

He was poised with his head just above the level of the eighth floor. In the distance the Sony was squawking, "Aw, you've got ring around the collar."

"Hold it," Barnie whispered over his shoulder. "He might reconnoiter during commercials."

"Yeah," Teresa whispered back, "he may even check out places."

But there was nothing. They strained to hear the slide and slap of carpet slippers under the Sony sound. Nothing. Barnie moved up past the last tread and stood under the TV & Sound Systems sign. A blue dot about a half block away was set like a sapphire among the dark, dead faces of TV screens. "Don't touch anything," Barnie murmured. "A lot of those sets are on rollers."

They moved down the center aisle. At last, past a display of rabbit-ear antennae, they could see the small square of the Sony screen. Midgets with tiny machine guns were wiping out Chicago on it and barreling off camera in little black Buicks.

The commercial was over, and now bullets were hailing, tires squealing, garbage cans crashing. Miniature mobsters were snarling threats. But there was a steady wheezing over this noise. The nightwatchman was stretched out in a Naugahyde recliner. He was holding a flashlight against his belly, like a school diploma. And he was sound asleep.

Barnie and Teresa backstepped all the way to the escalator, saying nothing till they were back on the Beds & Bedding level. "Let's not give way to optimism," Barnie muttered, "but he may be good for the whole night."

"They always turn up the volume for commercials," Teresa said. "One of them might wake him up sooner or later."

"Good point, so let's put a little distance between him and us. What are your instincts? We can't fight them all."

Teresa mentioned two: food and sleep.

"Sleep means back under the bed," Barnie said, "which won't give us our bearings. Food means . . . Where do they have food in a department store?"

"Candy's usually on the main floor."

"We start thinking like kids, we'll end up in a facility for kids."

"True," Teresa said. "And on a straight candy diet, we'd get sluggish and too big for under the bed. Macy's, though, they have food in their basement."

"But this isn't M—"

"I know, I know. But you got to start."

They waddled down like ducks, keeping their heads mostly lower than the level of the rubber banisters. "You counting the floors?"

"I think we're coming down to two—Junior Miss."

"You see the sign?"

"No. But if it's two, it's usually Junior Miss."

"What's Junior Miss?"

"My size. From a hair under Chubbette down to Petite."

The atmosphere changed when they crept halfway down to the main floor, as if they were climbing into a cathedral. The air was fresher, despite the aftersmell of French perfume. A couple of powder-blue lamps glowed in the distance. Main stretched out below them like a relief map of some incredibly rich country: Switzerland, but bigger.

"Welcome to Fantasy Island," Teresa murmured in awe. They squatted on the escalator steps, taking a rest. "There could be other nightwatchmen—other cats even," Teresa said.

"Maybe, maybe not," Barnie whispered. "We better keep moving, though." They got up and moved, down to the foot of the escalator, where a sign read,

*Be a darling and
pick up your poodle.*

and

Bare feet on the escalators is a no-no.

"More no-no's around here than a nursery school," Teresa mumbled.

"And it should be bare feet *are* a no-no," Barnie said, "if you got to say it at all."

Through the French perfume a faint smell of lox and cinnamon drifted up from the lower level. "Bingo," Teresa breathed.

They headed down the final flight of the escalator. It was like entering a mine, but there were distant lights that grew larger. Small colored lights clustered around a California Wines display of purple and yellow grape-shape bulbs wound into plastic leaves.

Even the sighing of sock feet echoed on the floor down there. They slid along, and the light from the glimmering grapes played over Barnie's lumber jacket. "What are we walking on?" Teresa said, lifting a foot.

They bent to see. The floor was tile with a pattern in it of a large fish, with scales, fins, eye, everything. "Chees," Teresa said, "I could eat *it*." They moved on.

"Let's not eat anything packaged unless it's open," Barnie said. "Tearing things open makes noise and leaves evidence. Let's exercise a little self-control."

"Don't push me past my limits," Teresa said. "But okay, aim toward deli."

"Where is it?"

58

"If you smell potato salad, move that way."

Darkness set in once they were past California Wines. The floor glowed dimly, but the counters were like hedges. Their hands moved out cautiously, over merchandise.

"We've gone in the wrong direction," Barnie said. "We're into Bargain Basement stuff."

"How can you tell?"

"I can't eat this." Barnie held up a carpet slipper in Teresa's face.

"This whole area smells like lint." They turned back, and Teresa ran her hand over a counter of Irregular Pantyhose. One of them bit her.

"Yeowww!"

Barnie's hand clamped over her mouth, stifling the scream. "You crazy?" he whispered.

"Something just bit me," Teresa gasped through his fingers. "I'm not hungry anymore. Let's go back to Bedding."

"Listen, keep your head. Nothing bit you. You're maybe hallucinating from hunger. You're starved and you know it. I'm starved. I know it."

"Listen, something in Pantyhose just bit me, I'm telling you."

Barnie patted the back of Teresa's coat. "It's dark down here, and we're under a lot of pressure—"

"You put *your* hand in Pantyhose and see what happens," she hissed back at him.

"Okay, okay," Barnie said. "It was probably just a staple on a package, but okay."

"Okay yourself if it makes you feel any better, but it was dripping fangs. It was probably a rattlesnake, and I've got six minutes to live. But let's get something to eat. Unless I'm really cracking up, I think I can smell Greek olive salad. Let's keep moving. If I got venom in my veins, I'd like to hurry it up and get it over with."

A dark aisle away they found the deli wavering behind long glass-covered counters. The whole place smelled like a Knights of Columbus picnic. Teresa was swallowing hard. Barnie followed her whisking coattail as she disappeared behind the counter, caught her toe on a raised wood floor, and sprawled below the cash register. She fell flat but had the presence of mind to say nothing. Wind gushed from her lungs. She struggled to speak.

"What did you say?" Barnie asked. She was still lying there, wheezing and fighting for breath.

"See . . . if . . . the . . . counter's unlocked. . . . If it is . . . look for those little . . . plastic cups . . . they . . . put . . . stuff in."

"Okay."

". . . And don't . . . be parti . . . cular. This is . . . survival . . . not a smorgasbord."

"Right." The back glass on the counter slid open, and mayo-flavored refrigerator air puffed out. Teresa could have cried.

A big spoon had been left in what might very well be rice pudding. Skimming evenly off the tops of the trays, Barnie began filling two cups.

"What are you getting?" Teresa asked from the floor.

"I'm not sure. I can't see, and the smells are all mixed up. I got here either herring in sour cream or bread pudding, and some other things too."

"Whatever," Teresa said.

In another minute Barnie squatted beside her and fitted a plastic cup into her hand. "You all right?"

She came up on an elbow, balancing the cup carefully. "Considering I may be a snakebite victim and I probably broke my nose falling over that platform thing, and I'm about to eat herring in sour cream or bread pudding but I don't know which, I'm not bad. You?"

"I been worse." Each grinned in the dark, hoping the other could see. The little plastic forks bent as they ate. Barnie rested back on his heels beside Teresa under the counter. "Basically it's herring in sour cream," he said, "which tends to kill your appetite before you really feel stuffed."

"Here," Teresa said, handing him something that seemed to come straight from her mouth. "You can put that back."

"You don't like cherry tomatoes?"

"Not if they're plastic."

"Oh yeah. I should have thought. It was over at the edge, like a trimming. I figured the parsley was paper, but—"

"No problem," Teresa said. "You did fine. If I'd been up there, I'd have lost my head and smeared rice pudding all over my body. You do good work, Barnie. It's us two against the world, right?"

"Looks like it," he said. "You want anything else to eat? Because if this was the herring, the other must be the rice pudding."

"No, I want to go to the powder room. There's got to be one around here somewhere."

"I don't know about that," Barnie said. "There may not—"

"I mean there's *got to be*," Teresa said, pulling herself up.

"Oh. Okay, but fight your instincts."

"Listen, Barnie, I'm only human, and if you don't have to go at this particular moment, you're going to some time."

"I don't mean that," he said. "I mean: don't flush."

Teresa rose blushing in the dark and felt her way in sock feet along to the side of the store. When she found the powder room, it'd be as dark as a pocket. Still those places are essentially alike. She'd manage.

The whole situation was unreal—doomed probably. If they made it through the night, they'd be lucky. Still Teresa felt about as good as she'd ever felt in her life. It was like she'd always hoped, like she'd just said and Barnie had almost agreed. It was the two of them against the world. Just the two of them, facing whatever came next.

What Teresa didn't know was that it hadn't been just the two of them. They hadn't been alone for a minute.

There'd been eyes on them the whole time. Eyes that saw better in the dark than theirs, and feet that moved softer. And minds that had already outthought the nightwatchman. Forbes & Ledsmar was dark and silent.

But it was far from empty.

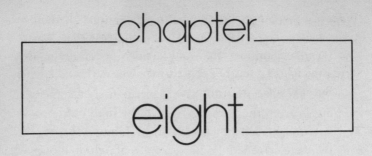

chapter

eight

At nine thirty, three electronic chimes on a timer sounded to start the Forbes & Ledsmar day. The store stirred. From every floor came the clank of cash drawers banging open.

On eight the Sony was cooling before an empty Naugahyde recliner. The nightwatchman had clocked out just ahead of the morning stampede of clerks. In Lower Level Hosiery, the cat, Pantyhose, rose from her nest of plastic packaging, spilled herself from the counter, and went looking for a quiet stockroom where she could sleep the day away. On seven, two pairs of shoes had vanished from under the queen-size bed.

In the last hour before dawn Barnie and Teresa had laid their morning plans. They were to split up and check the store out independently before meeting again at noon.

As the first of the sales personnel slumped to their posts, Barnie and Teresa drifted down side aisles, putting distance between themselves and the clerks and finally between each other.

At the far-off cattle-rush sound of the first customers ganging in from the parking lot and the mall entrance, Teresa found herself down on two in Junior Miss, reasonably well screened behind a rack of white glove-leather Windbreakers with suede piping and snakeskin flaps.

She was practically alone in a forest of drip-dry and leather-look. Except for one elderly salesperson who kept darting in and out of the stockroom behind a three-way mirror.

Teresa settled down to polish her just-browsing act, but her heart thudded under her coat, which was a distraction. Still, every time she caught a quick glimpse of the clerk, she felt a little calmer. On some of her trips from the stockroom the clerk staggered under a load of wraparound skirts higher than her head. Then on the return trips she seemed half-blind behind a pair of glasses with bottle-bottom lenses.

She was quite old, Teresa noticed, in spite of her patent-leather Mary Jane shoes and a weirdly youthful separates outfit. She also looked like the kind of saleslady who doesn't notice you until she has to. Teresa decided to risk a short stroll past a rack of Western-cut shirts and a swing through cashmere sweaters, casually checking prices like a customer.

Above a display case of ghastly plastic barrettes

Teresa stiffened. She sensed activity behind her. A whole group of people suddenly filled up the entrance to Junior Miss. Forcing herself to take her time, she made it back behind the rack of Windbreakers.

"And *where* is our Miss Filbert?" came a high-pitched voice, shattering the calm.

Between two Windbreakers Teresa could just see a top-heavy woman with raspberry-colored lips and incredibly black hair, standing with red-tipped claws on her hips. Behind her was a large crowd of what looked like college kids with poor posture.

"Miss Filbert?" the glass-cracking voice inquired again.

The clerk with the bottle-bottom glasses rounded from the stockroom, caught a Mary Jane on the side of the mirror, and mumbled a foul word.

Through the Windbreakers and over the clerk's shoulder Teresa watched the red-clawed woman expand, nearly blotting out the college types who were all carrying note pads in the store colors.

"Ah, *there's* our Junior Miss buyer, Miss Filbert!"

Teresa saw the bun on the back of Miss Filbert's head sink beneath her shoulders. "Here, Miss Filbert, is our newest crop of Merchandising Trainees on their first day of Orientation." The woman's raspberry lips curled in an official smile. "And I've been telling them that if anybody in the store can put them in the picture merchandise-wise, it's Our Miss Filbert of Junior Miss."

Miss Filbert's shoulders relaxed slightly. A pencil stuck through her bun teetered out and rolled down her back.

"All right, everybody," the trainee leader snapped, "crowd right into Junior Miss and notice how Miss Filbert has captured just the right *youthful* look for her department. All those posters of—who is that—Elvis Presley—Shaun Cassidy? Somebody. And the little psychedelic light that throws all those marvelous colors on the ceiling."

Teresa watched all the college creeps sniggering behind this woman who seemed to be the head honcho for sales personnel. The trainees were pointing at *Battlestar Galactica* appliqués and the plastic barrettes, rolling their eyes and poking each other.

"Well, Miss Filbert," said the honcho woman, "perhaps you could give this . . . group a *concise* overview of Junior Miss."

Miss Filbert shot a look at the stockroom door as if considering escape. But then she shrugged and turned her Fresca-bottle lenses on the college crowd. "Well, all right," she said. "How many of them are female?"

Four hands went up, and the rest of the group, taller, stared down at Miss Filbert with tired college eyes.

"Okay," she said vaguely. "Welcome to Junior Miss. We got clothing and accessorizing details here for the girl age twelve and up. We overlap to a degree with the Coeds College Bound Depart—"

"We'll do that department later," the honcho woman interrupted.

Miss Filbert turned on her. "You want to do it right now? Because, listen, I got more to do with my time around here than—"

"No, no. Go right on," the other woman said, jerking an earring loose from her lobe.

"Okay, where was I?" Miss Filbert sighed.

"Who knows?" came a deep voice from the back of the trainee group.

"Junior Miss is, hands down, the wors—most challenging department in Forbes and Ledsmar. Listen, if you make it here, you can make it anywhere. We dress these young . . . girls who haven't got any more taste and sense of style than . . ."

Miss Filbert seemed to dry up suddenly, and Teresa followed her gaze. With dim vision Miss Filbert had caught sight of one of the trainees who was standing near the front of the group in a Jaws II T-shirt over a tie-dyed skirt. She was cracking gum and scratching one bare leg with the other wedgie. Even to Teresa she was a pretty gross spectacle. Miss Filbert's glasses crept down her nose. "Let's see, where was I?"

"Who—"

"Oh yeah. We spot the junior-high and high-school trends and stock the stuff before any other mall store in the area. We also deal with the older grade-school girl. These days, some of them are the size of Godzilla—"

The honcho woman cleared her throat.

Miss Filbert reached for the pencil at the back of her head and failed to find it. "Where was—so like one season it's all denim. Then denim's out, and what you don't sell goes back to the manufacturer. You talk about a hassle.

"Then the next season it's all skirts with fly fronts, and then the teen-agers are back to denim just when you're really into leather. Or maybe *they're* Fonzie Fifties, and *you're* Funky Forties.

"They don't know what they want. And when their mothers come in here and try to buy anything for them, you can kiss that sale off, because the girls just bring the stuff back. I've had merchandise back in here that looks like it went through a wreck on the turnpike."

"Perhaps," said the other woman, expanding again until her employee's I.D. tag hung well away from her upper body, "if instead of *telling,* you could *show*—"

"You want show?" Miss Filbert said. "I'll give you show." Teresa shrank behind the Windbreakers, but Miss Filbert made a sudden lunge in the other direction. "Now here, for instance, we've been pushing Western-cut shirts. We call it the Dale Evans look."

The trainee group snorted openly, and the pathetic figure in the aged Jaws II T-shirt stared in a daze, cracking her gum like gunfire.

"Okay," said Miss Filbert, "so it didn't really take off. But it could catch on right at the end of the season. We do a lot of camp business."

"The whole thing's camp," said the Jaws II T-shirt.

69

"I'm talking *summer* camp, Smart Mouth," Miss Filbert spat.

The honcho woman cleared her throat again. "But what I meant by *show,* dear Miss Filbert, was this. Perhaps you could locate a young customer and just talk us through a typical Sales Situation."

Miss Filbert twitched. "You see a young customer in the department? Because I don't——"

Teresa froze in horror as the red-lipped woman flowed suddenly toward the Windbreaker rack. In a single gesture she parted the jackets, which jangled back on their hangers. A price tag for $139.95 leaped out of Teresa's hand. Nothing stood between her and the two women and the crowd of trainees. Eyes were all over her. Instinct urged flight, but she was numb to the knees.

Miss Filbert elbowed the other woman out of the way and gave Teresa a hard look through her goggles. Teresa caught a reflection of herself in the powerful lenses. The hanging threads from the scooped-off buttons on her coat from yesterday's adventure in the collapsing building. The slacks beneath, covering her numb legs in a polyester pattern of brown-and-beige argyle dulled by time. Teresa could even see her own shoes, which looked like Minnie Mouse but were actually recycled from her aunt. Miss Filbert never looked above Teresa's neck. At least she didn't get a fix on my face, she thought.

"Ye gods," Miss Filbert remarked.

The merchandising trainees stared at Teresa in

mingled pity and disgust. It was a college-type look. She'd seen it before.

Miss Filbert breathed deeply. "Okay, kid," she said, "just step around those Windbreakers, and let's have a better look at you."

"I wasn't—"

"I know, I know." Miss Filbert turned her lenses up on the trainee leader. "I think this is a hopeless case," she hissed none too quietly.

"Nonsense!" said the leader, smiling hideously. "I'm sure we can do something with this . . . damsel in distress." She turned on the trainee group. "Take notes," she barked.

And then she returned to Teresa, who hadn't moved because the woman had her arm in a grip. "I'm sure you wouldn't mind a little assistance with your selections, would you, precious?"

"Y—no," Teresa said, feeling very pale.

"And your mother's shopping with you today, is she, dearest?"

"N—yes," Teresa answered.

"Possibly she's up in the Better Dresses department?" Teresa looked thoughtful at this possibility.

"Why aren't you in school, kid?" the Jaws II trainee shot at her.

"Why aren't you?" Teresa shot back.

"Isn't she darling?" the trainee leader asked, giving her a sudden shake. "Now let's just get that—coat off and see if we have any particular figure problems." Underneath, Teresa was wearing a gray athletic-department sweat shirt over her polyester slacks. The leader flinched.

"Well, yes," she smiled over her shoulder at her chain gang, "after all, the training bra *is* a thing of the past, I suppose." She turned back on Teresa. "Tell me, sweetie, do you go to a really laid-back school, mix-and-match-wise?"

Don't show fear, Barnie'd said when they split up for safety at nine thirty. *Whatever situation you get into, don't show fear. And keep moving if you can. And meet me at noon in Underwear.* The trainee leader had her in half a hammerlock hug again, so she could follow only half of Barnie's advice. "I guess you could say we mix and match pretty much at my school."

The woman's sudden smile illuminated all of Junior Miss. "Now here we have the textbook case to the practiced eye. This young lady goes to a terribly smart suburban school. It never fails, the more fashionable the school, the tacki—the more casually they dress. These more affluent suburban youngsters—" she was talking straight at the Jaws II trainee now—"could buy and sell us all. They have nothing, simply nothing to prove fashion-wise." She whirled back on Teresa again like a striking reptile. "Where do you go to school, honey, Saddle River?"

"How'd you know?" Teresa said, perfectly.

"Got it in one!" the leader crowed. "I nearly said Short Hills—silly me! But of course I wouldn't have been far wrong. I never am."

She seemed to fling Teresa away again without let-

72

ting go of her. "Here lies our challenge," she told the trainees. "We must lead these affluent, confused youngsters into Patron Patterns that will carry them right on through to the better colleges and of course beyond. Naturally she'll need more . . . guidance than JM alone. She'll need makeup hints, but that's down on main. And Styling Like Sassoon is up on nine for her hair. But we must do our bit."

Teresa blacked out somewhat in the next half hour. She had the sensation of people dealing with her body while her mind sort of floated away: all the way past Saddle River, wherever that was.

The whole thing was similar to a tonsillectomy. She knew they were working her over, but her mind was on a dimmer. Somebody wrenched her arm getting her into a blouse. There was some business with a lamb's-wool pullover that went on and came off. And somebody was doing up buttons on her, which reminded her of snowsuits.

Somebody else wound a wraparound skirt onto her, which was a little like being hanged by the waist until you're dead.

Then an unmistakable voice said, "There now, sweetie, you can just sort of step out of your—slacks. We've got you decently covered."

Teresa's mind cleared somewhat as she pulled her shoes out of her slacks. As they led her to the three-way mirror, she noticed flickers of interest in the vacant eyes of the college crowd. Miss Filbert was telling everybody not to mess up her merchandise.

Then Teresa was standing at the mirror, looking at three of herself. She had on a good-looking white blouse, real cotton. Her old athletic-department sweat shirt peeped out in a triangle through the collar, and the whole effect wasn't half bad. The wraparound skirt was a nice rich green, like fir trees. "Gives her a little color," said the voice, "and heaven knows, she needs it." Her shoes were still her aunt's. "We'll just have to overlook the footgear," the familiar voice said, "but, Miss Filbert, could you manage socks? Any matching pair will be a great improvement."

Not half-bad at all, Teresa thought. The last new thing she'd had was a pair of Levi's that hadn't worked out because she'd sat in the bathtub with them on. The idea had been to get them to shape to her, but they ended up shaped like the bathtub.

Blades flashed at her elbow, and she shied. In the mirrors she watched a trio of Miss Filberts attacking her with scissors. "That's right, Miss Filbert, let's just get those manufacturers' tags off."

The trainee leader was lecturing her group on the finer points. "The important thing is to get a total outfit *on the Young Customer's back.*"

She was whispering to the group, but Teresa could hear it all. "And select for her a terribly basic all-over Look. Then she can dress it down if she goes to one of the better schools. And, of course, she can dress it up if she comes from one of the changing neighborhoods or any place pushy. The thing is *get something on her and get her charge card.*

74

"You have a charge card, don't you, darling?" Six red lips smiled down at her in the three-way mirror.

"Not on me," Teresa said.

"Ah! Mummy doesn't let you wander around with your own card!" She shot a knowing look back at the trainees. "Prudent woman. Nevertheless, dear, you just run up to Better Dresses and show Mummy your marvelous transformation. She's bound to be . . . overjoyed."

"But—" said Teresa.

"No buts about it, darling. Run on up to Mummy, and tell her to drop by Junior Miss and flash us her card."

"But—" Miss Filbert said, before the trainee leader stunned her with a look.

Here was an invitation to run along, but Teresa couldn't quite get off the starting mark. For one thing she was transfixed by her images. Really, she repeated to herself, she didn't look half-bad. The shoes looked pretty wretched now, but matching socks made a difference. On the other hand she didn't have a Mummy in Better Dresses, and as for a charge card . . .

"Run along, dearest," the trainee leader hissed. "We'll just . . . dispose of your . . . coat and those . . . slacks, shall we?"

"Might as well," Teresa said, and stepping very carefully, she ran along.

chapter

nine

Barnie'd said to meet him in Underwear, which Teresa took to mean Men's & Boys'. She drifted down to main and past Designer Neckties & Pocket Handkerchiefs. Hanging a left at Cuff Links, she felt the pleasant sway of the wraparound skirt. Not half-bad, she repeated, passing the Brut Boutique and Soaps on Ropes. "Smell like a Man," read a life-size poster of Pete Rose, and Teresa rolled her eyes.

She found Barnie staring up at a display of Jockey shorts in Hawaiian Hues. When he saw Teresa, he stepped back against Drip-Dry Ultra Briefs. "What happened to you?"

"Too much to explain here," Teresa said. Everywhere she looked were elasticized waistbands and fly fronts. "Let's go for some lunch."

"Dream on," Barnie said.

"No," she said. "I think they'll feed us."

"Look, survival's one thing. Theft's another. Besides, they can't make you return food." Barnie looked worried. "Can they?"

"I know, I know," Teresa said. "Still I can fight my instincts, but I can't fight theirs. What you don't buy, they make you take."

She explained a little of what she'd just been through in Junior Miss on their way up the escalator.

On nine, opposite the Styling-Like-Sassoon Salon, was the Renaissance Room for Midday Dining. A double line of shoppers was waiting for tables all the way back to the powder room. "Get a place in line," Teresa said. She wanted to duck in the powder room to get her hair and face more in line with her new outfit. Just soap and water, and a comb if they had one.

"What a sexist pig of a place this store is," Barnie grumbled.

"Meaning what?"

"Meaning there's a so-called powder room on every floor, and exactly two men's rest rooms in the whole place, and one of them's Employees Only. I know. I used them both."

"Did you wash your neck and ears?"

"Very funny."

Faced with this grumpiness, Teresa ducked back to the powder room, which was embarrassingly handy.

When she got back, Barnie was practically at the head of the line, and a hostess gripping menus was just on the other side of a velvet rope. "Look," he muttered to Teresa, "I don't think this is going to work. They may want to see our charge card. See that cashier over in that little box? She looks like a kill-crazed rhino."

She did. Teresa wasn't even hungry anymore. "I guess I can make it till midnight," she whispered. "But this time let's go for the rice pudd—"

An immense woman parted the Single Diners line of standees and stepped across. She was wearing a yellow wig and carrying a big purse that swung from her elbow. "If you kids are in the Two and More line, how about if I'm More? I got no time to hang around in Single Diners."

Teresa stared at her. She was one big woman. Wet sweat lines zigzagged down her face from wrinkle to wrinkle. "Look, I'm a busy woman," she said.

Barnie made an incredible little bow. "Be our guest," he said up at her and then turned his palms out. Teresa nodded.

The hostess could barely keep ahead of this woman who flowed across the Renaissance Room like lava. Teresa and Barnie followed. Crystal chandeliers dripped all over the room, but Teresa had no time to drink in the atmosphere. Her appetite seemed to have left her for good. She could tell that the hostess and the big woman were carrying on some rapid-fire conversation, but she couldn't catch any of it.

The woman flopped into the center of a curving booth, and the buttoned plastic cushions sighed. There was just room for Teresa and Barnie on either side of her. They sat tilted at sharp angles, leaning in her direction as the cushions bottomed out. The woman grabbed three menus out of the hostess's hand, saying, "Yeah, yeah. Get outta here."

She slammed bifocals on a chain onto her nose. But she didn't even open her menu, which was in a fuzzy paper folder that reminded Teresa of *The Velveteen Rabbit*. The woman was scanning the room. "Trouble over there," she said to herself. And as far as Teresa could tell, she was staring holes in two very respectable women in pants suits eating cottage cheese.

In fact she was working the whole room with her eyes. Barnie peered around her chins at Teresa and tapped a finger on his temple. Maybe she was crazy, Teresa thought. Maybe not. She seemed pretty definite in her ideas, whatever they were.

"Wouldja look at that?" the woman said, digging Teresa's ribs. "Plastic flowers. Every table. Plastic, and take a look at the prices. They oughtta call this place the Rip-Off Room."

The prices seemed a bigger problem than the plastic lilacs on their table to Teresa, but the woman was talking again. "Yeah, yeah, so why do I eat here? Because if you ever ate in the Employees' Cafeteria, you wouldn't ask, so don't ask."

Teresa could see Barnie shrink on the far side. "You . . . work in the store?" he said faintly.

But the big woman didn't seem to hear him. She was

fingering a sprouting mole on her jaw, deep in concentration. Her eyes were boring into a little old woman seated over by the salad bar. She was a nice-looking old woman with a veil thing over blue hair and a grandmother bracelet, flashing disks. "Fingers Ferguson," the big woman observed. "Double trouble."

She drew herself up suddenly, and ice water swayed in goblets all over the room. "My only drawback is I'm too dedicated," she said. "Can't unwind." The tablecloth churned as her big legs eased apart, threatening to bat Teresa and Barnie out of the booth.

"I'm married to my job. I'm probably an ulcer case and don't know it. I'll have the patty melt plate with fries."

Teresa looked up to find a waitress there, dressed like a French gypsy in a foot-high starched headdress. "No, I don't know what fancy name you got for it. Just gimme the patty melt and fries. And swap the green salad for baked beans. Coffee to go. I don't have all day."

"The same," Teresa said.

"Make that three," Barnie said, his voice fainter than ever.

Want to make a run for it? Barnie mouthed silently when the big woman went back to scanning the room. Teresa got the message in a single reading but didn't know what to do with it. She looked at the woman's hands. They were the size of catcher's mitts, patting out a heavy rhythm on the tablecloth. Teresa concentrated on a loose thread on her new skirt and shook her head. Barnie slumped.

"Lucky for me you kids were in line when I come along," the woman boomed suddenly. "I don't eat, I lose my strength. I probably got the metabolism of some weedy little woman and don't know it. My name's Small—"

Teresa's eyes bulged out.

"—Bertha Small, but you can call me Bertha. I got a couple grandchildren around your age," she said. "Somewhere. Anybody see us three here in the booth probably take me for your grandmother."

True, Teresa thought, which will get us through maybe twenty minutes more of life if things go just right.

"And don't tell me it's some school holiday. I know kids today. They oughtta put revolving doors on the schoolhouses. You're in—you're out—you go—you don't go. Boy, in my day it was different. But don't worry about me. I got bigger fish to fry." Teresa was trying to follow this train of thought in case there was a threat at the end of it when a question from Bertha paralyzed her. "What school you go to anyhow when you go?"

"Ever hear of Saddle River?" Teresa said with some care. Barnie looked around Bertha's mammoth front and stared.

"Fancy-schmancy," Bertha remarked. "Boy, what I wouldn'ta given for your advantages."

The food was set in front of them, and Barnie began doing a convincing imitation of a condemned man eating his last meal. Bertha raised her hamburger bun and stared under it. "Hey," she yelled out to the retreating waitress, "I ordered a patty melt, not a Brillo pad!" The waitress sped through a swinging door.

The fries on her plate wafted Teresa's appetite back, but she wasn't going to be able to swallow with this kind of suspense hanging over her. "Say, Bertha, what line of work are you in?"

Bertha worked a tongue around her lower plate. "Ever hear of the CIA?"

The fork in Barnie's baked beans seemed to keel out of the dish and go skittering across the tablecloth. "I'm sort of this store's CIA. Undercover stuff," Bertha boomed. "Very hush-hush."

Why did I ask? Teresa thought, tackling her patty melt anyway. They ate in silence, but fast, watching Bertha's chewing face pan the Renaissance Room like a monitoring device.

Teresa was just poking at a ketchup blob with her last fry when Bertha snapped suddenly to attention. Barnie threw up a protective arm and closed his eyes. The vase of plastic lilacs went over.

"Let me outta here, kids!" Bertha yelled.

Teresa took the full force of a giant elbow in her stomach and found herself sitting on the carpet. Barnie was trying to go leg over leg the other way. Bertha rose up, and the table fought for balance. She stepped over

Teresa, and her purse whistled through the air. She threw back the flap on it and grabbed out a green cloud of dollar bills. Teresa saw an official-looking silver badge pinned to the inside of the flap.

"Stand aside!" Bertha was thundering, and Teresa looked up from the floor. The hostess, a tall, quivering column of pink Ultrasuede, tried to block Bertha's way. "I left the money," Bertha said. "It'll pay for me and the kids. I got a fix on Fingers—"

"Please, Bertha," the hostess was breathing, "*not* in my dining room."

"Got no time, got no time. I got a sure collar," Bertha said, charging away across the room.

Teresa sat on the carpet, still dazed. Somewhere above her Barnie was saying, "That take care of it?"

And the hostess replied, "I suppose it will have to. Nothing for the tip, naturally. And if you happen to be a . . . relative or something of Bertha's, *please* tell her to use the EC—the Employees' Cafeteria. I'm trying to maintain a certain *tone* in the dining room."

Barnie got Teresa to her feet, and they weaved their way between the tables. "This is just what we don't want," Barnie muttered. "A lot of attention."

"Who'll remember *us?*" Teresa said out loud. "They've just watched Bertha barrel through here like she was invading Poland. Her purse alone must weigh forty pounds. You see what was pinned on the inside of it?"

"I saw."

They took the escalators all the way down to main, not speaking till they got there. "Well," Barnie said, "anyhow, we ate."

"I hope I can keep it down," Teresa said. "My nerves are about shot."

"Let's get out of the store a little while. We could do with a change. I'm feeling a little rocky myself."

They headed past Evening Bags to the parking-lot entrance. The automatic doors were sliding back and forth. Beyond the puffs of perfume they could faintly smell the world. Teresa stopped short. Outside, autumn sunlight glared off a thousand windshields and glazed the blacktop.

"Chees," she said, pulling back, "I'd forgotten about weather."

chapter

ten

They stood blinking out at the blacktop. In the distance they could just make out a figure weaving between the Cordobas and the Sevilles.

It looked like an oversize praying mantis, and it flowed like a surfer. As it swept nearer, Teresa saw it was somebody in cutoffs and knee warmers, a girl because she had on an elastic top. She was riding a skateboard and wearing headphones clamped over both ears. She still looked like a bug, but bigger: something intelligent but brutal from science fiction. Up and down the rows she skimmed, following the arrows on the asphalt. She seemed to be patrolling the lot.

"So what would we do out there?" Teresa asked. The

asphalt wavered off into infinity, not even climate controlled.

"I guess you're right. We've sort of turned our backs on all that."

"I mean one day," Teresa said, "even today maybe—they'll blow the whistle on us, and we'll be back out there again. Who's in a hurry?"

They backtracked a department or two and angled through Active Sportswear. As they approached the dark doors that led to covered parking, they saw a crowd. "What do we do about mobs?" Teresa said. "Keep out or melt in?"

Barnie shrugged, and they moved to the edge of the crowd where they could go either way. Being smaller, Barnie slipped into a grove of limbs holding shopping bags. He was back beside Teresa in the next moment. He led her away by the arm.

"What's happening?"

"A bad scene," he mumbled.

"How bad could it be? Somebody try to drive into the store?"

"Naw, I'd just as soon forget it."

"Then I'm going back and see for my—"

"All right, all right." Barnie gripped her arm tighter. "It was Bertha doing her thing, if you have to know everything. So okay, we already knew she was a plain-clotheswoman, even if we didn't exactly spell it out to each other. She caught that little old lady with the blue hair taking something out of the store."

Teresa glanced down at her new Pima cotton shirt

with the mother-of-pearl buttons and double-stitched pocket flaps. "And?"

"Bertha had her down on the floor, and the old lady was wiggling around, and a lot of stuff was spilling out of a shopping bag, but Bertha was all over her."

"So," Teresa said, "she got a collar on Fingers Ferguson."

"Don't talk so rough," Barnie said.

The only other doors led to the mall. Beyond, indoor trees waved gently in the air conditioning: sugar maples and coconut palms, mixed. "We should have thought of this first," Teresa said. "It's a change of scene, but not so . . ."

"Radical," Barnie said.

They were just past the Smoking Is a No-No sign when Teresa saw the boy. She'd never seen a boy like this particular one, who was stepping in front of her, almost cutting her off.

He was tall, but not gangly, lean but not skinny. Blond hair, lightly styled, waved down just to his shirt collar. A little peach fuzz glowed on his cheeks. And he was wearing knife-creased gray flannels and a double-breasted navy blue blazer that fit like a glove.

The boy was walking ahead of them, side-stepping the baby strollers and striding with purpose through the wandering crowds. Teresa couldn't tear her gaze away from him. She was walking faster, nudging ambling Barnie along past Hoffritz for Cutlery and a line of really dreary boutiques.

Just opposite the Karmelkorn Kastle the blazer boy

pivoted on his heel and mounted the bridge arching the artificial creek. He stood there at the highest point, and Teresa caught a glimpse of his profile. He seemed to be looking back at her and Barnie.

They moved on past him, but Teresa felt the boy's eyes on her. Ahead of them the mall's main intersection was looming up. The artificial creek went underground beneath a large plaza. In the center of it was some big sculpture made out of chrome-plated tractor parts. Directional signs pointed to where the mall split into a major walkway toward K mart and a shorter stroll toward Cinema I and II.

They started in a wide circle around the sculpture. Barnie jerked a thumb down the K mart walkway, past a lot of signs: DISCOUNT-O-RAMA, FACTORY-2-U, BAR-GAIN BONANZA, MULCH CITY CUT-RATE GARDENING SUPPLIES. "You want to—"

"Naw," Teresa said, "it's not much of a neighborhood."

Barnie beetled his brow up at her. "Boy, you've come a long way in less than a day."

But instead of feeling guilty inside her new outfit, she only thought Barnie's lumber jacket was a little . . . out of place. Not grubby, necessarily, just a little—

The boy in the blazer was coming up from behind. Teresa sensed him gaining on them just before she caught a flash of blue blazer out of the corner of her eye. He slowed as he came even with them, then dropped behind. They'd circled the plaza and were heading back

88

toward Forbes & Ledsmar before she really lost him. When she looked back, pretending to examine a window display of Candles in Shapes You Never Thought Of, he wasn't there at all. And yet she had the feeling that he wasn't far away.

Barnie seemed to be though—at least in his thoughts. Teresa elbowed him as they wandered along by the creek. "You get the feeling we're being watched?" she muttered.

"I did," Barnie said. "When we were checking out the parking lot. I had the feeling someone was checking *us* out. That big bug-shaped girl with the headphones and the skateboard. I couldn't see her eyes, but I sort of felt them. Know what I mean?"

Teresa did. But it was the blazer boy's eyes she'd felt. "I guess we're getting jumpy. A person would in our situation." They trudged on, back into the store. Teresa waved the perfume lady aside, absentmindedly.

Teresa and Barnie lay under the queen-size, a floor below the late movie. Their shoes were lined up by their feet, and Teresa was half-asleep. She'd caught a few winks between nine thirty and midnight, but she could use a few more. It wasn't to be though.

"I wish that cat would get used to us," Barnie whispered. "She had her nose right in my ear. You hungry? Teresa, you hungry?"

"Not much," she said, "if it means going all the way down to Gourmet. You?"

89

"I could eat, but we've got all night. Or anyway till the movie's over. But I don't think it's a good policy to stay under here a lot."

"Why not?"

"For one thing, you can't see your hand in front of your face. That bedspread cuts whatever light there is."

"So what's to see?"

"That's the point. We're blind as moles. We ought to get our eyes adjusted to the rest of the store for safety's sake. Besides, I'm getting a crick in my neck. We stay on this floor every night, and we're liable to get arthritis."

Teresa groaned. "Barnie, arthritis is not pillow talk. Nobody who's trying to get some sleep after a busy day likes to hear the person next to her carrying on about arthritis."

But he'd made his point. Teresa was bolt awake. The bed springs were three inches from her nose, so she couldn't even shift around to get comfortable. But it didn't matter. Barnie was already edging out from under the bed, stirring up dust.

In another minute or so they were sidling in sock feet to the escalator. "You want to hit the deli?" Barnie whispered.

"Let's make a stop on two first," Teresa answered. "The Varsity Shop, I think they call it. It's next to Junior Miss."

"What for?"

"Get you some new clothes. That lumber jacket of yours is going to stand up by itself one of these days."

90

"Now wait a minute, I'm not—"

The escalator was nearer than they'd remembered. There was a moment of blank silence up on eight.

But it was only a station break. The nightwatchman's snore rumbled on, carrying over into a commercial. "You're soaking in it," came a tiny tinny voice. They started down.

Rounding four, Barnie continued. "Nothing wrong with this lumber jacket. I'm not going to take a lot of—"

"Not *take*," Teresa explained. "*Borrow.* I been giving it some thought. We can't go around in the same stuff all the time. We'd be too easy to spot, and did you see a Laundromat around here? No. So I'm going back to Junior Miss and return this shirt *which they made me take if you remember.* And I'm going to put it back. Then I'm going to take—borrow another. I mean with just a day's wearing, it isn't even shopworn. They can sell it or push it off on somebody else like they pushed it off on me. I figure I'll recycle skirts every other day. Likewise socks."

"Yeah?" Barnie said. "What about the stuff you put back? There won't be tags on it."

"They never get around to tagging everything."

"I don't know," Barnie said as they crept through Tall Girls. "I never had any new clothes before. Brand new."

"Well, here's your chance." Through a dim archway hanging in triangles that Teresa remembered were college pennants, the Varsity Shop appeared. In a professional voice Teresa began to chant, "Here we cater to the Young Boy, twelve years and older. *Basically* the junior-and-senior-high set, though some of the grade-school boys these days are as big as Godzil—"

"Can it," Barnie muttered.

They stood in the center of the Varsity Shop rug, which seemed to be horse-blanket plaid. A display of cable-knit crew necks was arranged on hunting horns. There were blazers too, Teresa noticed, clumped to-gether on a rack. A dummy in the corner was wearing a navy blue one. She stared at it, lost in thought. Then, to give Barnie a nudge, she murmured, "I think they're having Incredible Reductions in chinos."

"Chees," he said. "First you encourage me to steal; now you're helping me find a bargain. Why don't you just go on ahead to Junior Miss or wherever and change your shirt."

Teresa slunk off, somewhat stung.

She wondered why men are so touchy on the subject of their clothes—snap your head off when you're only trying to help. It must be some basic difference in the sexes. She spotted the rack of white glove-leather Wind-breakers, which helped her get her bearings. Where were shirts from here? Her hand moved over a counter top, but it was the wrapping desk. Nothing there but a pair of scissors. She located a rack, but when she got up close enough, she saw it was that Dale Evans West-ern junk.

She hit pay dirt at the next rack, which seemed to feature shirts and sweaters as coordinates. Why not?

Teresa thought. She slipped out of her shirt and eased a fresh one off the hanger. It was a reasonable fit, cut a little full, but with a sweater . . .

She picked out a dark one, something plain and unnoticeable. None of that patterned novelty stuff for me, she thought. Too obvious. I got to dress it way down. As she pulled the sweater over her head, she was absolutely blind for a moment, enveloped in the pleasant scent of new clothes.

Then in a sort of reflex action, Teresa headed to the three-way mirror, which was as dark as the mouth of a cave. She stared into the blank glass for a few seconds and then gave it up. She was just turning to go back for the scissors to get the tags off the clothes when she noticed a dress dummy she could have sworn hadn't been there before.

It seemed to be a perfect plastic version of a Junior Miss Young Customer with tight gold curls and a sickeningly sweet smile painted on its glossy mouth. One hard little arm was crooked at the waist. The other pointed out from a little bent wrist the way store dummies are always posed.

Eerie, Teresa thought. Then she noticed the figure was wearing a nice neutral-colored blouse with full sleeves under a V-necked sleeveless sweater. The layered look, Teresa thought, but is it me? The dummy seemed to grin at her. Only the eyes under the false lashes looked glassy and dead.

Wonder if that sweater's cashmere, Teresa asked herself, stepping near to finger the V-neck. The dummy

93

teetered on its pedestal. "Holy—!" Teresa made a grab at the thing to keep it from crashing over on the floor.

The thing grabbed back.

Teresa opened her mouth to scream. But the hard little hand clamped it shut. The other hard little hand closed over her wrist and flipped her in a judo movement. Teresa spun in the air, shrieking silently, and ended on her knees. Her wraparound skirt was wrapped around her head, and her arm was forced steadily up her back, crackling and popping. She considered passing out with the pain. Shock was moving over her in waves, and she still couldn't scream because of the hard little half-human hand. A hard little knee now drove into her lower back, threatening her kidneys. She was sinking lower and lower onto the floor, heaving with horror behind the hand. Red pain branched all over her body, but still she couldn't yell to warn—

The hard little hand eased up on her arm. She could lift her head under the tent of her skirt to see across the gray and black Junior Miss floor. Everything was faintly outlined except the . . . thing that still gripped her. She could see—

Barnie. She could recognize his shape. He was standing by the Dale Evans shirts, and he seemed to be holding something in his cupped hands. But no, that wasn't it. His hands were tied together at the wrists with a Varsity Shop belt. A Pierre Cardin probably, Teresa thought, going a little crazy.

Looming over Barnie with hands on his shoulders was a familiar figure. She knew who it was at once. She could see the bright glow on the blond hair that waved down to the collar. The darkness below was a fitted blue blazer. It looked like another clothes dummy, but it wasn't. It was the boy who'd tracked them on their stroll out of the store. *He* was alive all right. And she knew he'd nabbed Barnie before poor old Barn had had a chance to change his clothes because the blue-blazer boy's hands were digging into Barnie's shoulders, near his neck, bunching up the old lumber jacket.

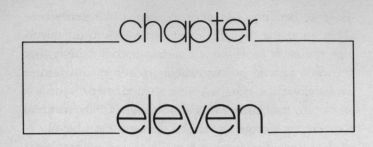

chapter

eleven

It was a nightmare, and it wouldn't quit. Teresa was being frog-marched up the fire stairs with a bobby sock rammed in her mouth, and to keep it there, a designer silk scarf was knotted at the back of her neck.

By the red light at each landing she could see the blazer boy hoisting Barnie along ahead of her. Barnie was gagged with something that looked like a striped tank top. Two shoulder straps hung down his back. But she couldn't see the . . . girl—yes, it was a living girl and not a dress dummy—who was digging her in the back up every step.

Bertha I could deal with, is all Teresa could think. Harley Probst and the Kobras even. Anybody, but not—

They were back up on seven and moving through a swinging door out of the stairwell. Teresa sensed that

Beds & Bedding was over to their right somewhere. That's fine, she thought, just take us back to the queen-size and leave us. If we just all hang a right about now.

But the blond guy was snapping a finger in Barnie's face and veering left, past what seemed to be Daybeds & Recliners, into Furniture & Furnishings. Unknown territory, Teresa thought, even if she could see it better.

And then the blazer guy was slowing Barnie down, weaving around shin-high, nearly invisible slabs. The four of them moved on through a minefield of cocktail tables, or something low. And then they slipped off deeper into the shadows past Conversational Modules. Teresa's tongue went dry trying to work around a mouthful of ribbed cotton.

A blue-flannel forearm slammed Barnie to a halt, and Teresa slammed into Barnie's back. And still there was this incredible, complete silence. They were human, those other two, but they moved like Darth Vader. Teresa and Barnie stood there, staring into a display of Machine-Washable Drapes.

The blond guy must have given a signal because the drapes parted. Teresa watched Barnie being nudged forward till his nose was up against another set of drapes, heavier. She stumbled after him, with only a small jab in the ribs from the hard little hand to move her.

The drapes behind closed, and the drapes ahead opened. Teresa flinched when a hand swatted the back of Barnie's head. But she staggered after him, farther and farther into blackness, into the unknown.

Teresa managed to stop, weaving a little to keep from falling down. She was standing ankle deep in carpeting. With any luck this meant they weren't about to blunder into an open elevator shaft. Lights went on, and Teresa was blinded all over again, but only in the first moment.

All four of them were in the middle of a room. A real room, almost, not a department. A room set up for living, except that all the furniture had tags on it. A room full of furniture, and—yes—human figures.

There was a fake fireplace at the far end, with a couple of matching love seats on either side. There were people sitting in the love seats, unmoving. Teresa's eyes skated away. There was a drop-leaf table in front of a fake window. A doorway seemed to lead to another room, and who knows what or who might be in there.

She concentrated on Barnie. She watched him make a slow turn, his eyes bulging at this fancy room full of furniture and—

He caught sight of her with the silk scarf wrapped around her mouth. Her eyes were probably rolling like a mad horse. She watched his gaze shift to the girl beside her, the girl who still had her by the upper arm. Teresa caught a glimpse of a curly gold head but dared not see more.

She looked down at the white shag carpeting instead. But there was the worst sight of all. A dark figure sprawled there against the white. A figure slick and spidery. Teresa shrieked soundlessly into the bobby sock.

And the eyes were on her, from every corner of the room, unreal eyes watching her silent screaming.

The girl with the grip and the gold curls stood patiently beside her, waiting for Teresa to calm down a little. Her grip loosened by degrees and then fell away from Teresa's arm. But she could see the hard little hand at the end of a blousy sleeve. It was coiled into a tiny fist, ready for anything. And the little girl curls looked ready to spring. And now Teresa's head was turning, and she was looking at her, at the little glittering eyes in the flawless face. The little eyes weren't dead anymore beneath the false lashes.

The eyes bored into Teresa, driving her past panic. I think that V-neck *is* cashmere, Teresa thought, going crazy again. But a little pink tongue came out of the girl's lacquered lips and ran a narrow moist line over the Cupid's bow. At last she was going to speak.

It was a very soft voice, strangely sweet. "Now then," it said, "we're going to take your gags off in just a moment." She looked at the blazer boy who was hovering near Barnie. "Aren't we, Ken?"

He cocked an aristocratic eyebrow at her and nodded.

"But before we do," she went on, "I want to make something just as clear to you both as I possibly, possibly can, okay?" Teresa felt herself nod.

"Okay." The girl gave her a little comforting half-smile. "You're on our turf," she murmured, still smiling. "You have absolutely no rights whatever. Because you are not one of us."

99

The girl looked all the way down the length of Teresa, and her eyes drifted over to Barnie's lumber jacket. "We will dispose of you," the girl went on, "in any way we choose. But we are very fair, and everyone in our little . . . society is an equal. Except of course for me. I am more equal than the others. But you two—" Her terrifying, glittering gaze swept over Barnie again, though it was really Teresa she was giving the business to, "are not our equals at all.

"One of our little rules should be obvious even to you. We never, never, never raise our voices. Is that understood?" Teresa watched Barnie's tank-topped face nodding. "And so before we remove the gags, remember that if you even make the tiniest little squeak without being given permission to speak, I'll slap the living—"

The blazer boy—Ken—cleared his throat. They stepped up to Teresa and Barnie. The girl jerked away the silk square along with a handful of Teresa's hair. Teresa opened her mouth to howl, but the smiling girl had one hand in the air, palm open. Teresa swallowed loose threads and watched Barnie spitting out something like white elastic onto the white carpet. This can't be happening, Teresa said, but not out loud.

The belt was whipped off Barnie's wrists, leaving welts. The blazer boy smiled down at him, seeming to say: just try something, you pathetic wimp.

The girl had left Teresa's side. She was moving gracefully over to the drop-leaf table, stepping behind it. She stood there in front of the fake window, which was a photographic blowup of a village with thatched cottages. She made little tripods of her hands on the tabletop.

"Now then," she said, barely audible, "I call this meeting to order."

Figures from all over the room moved into a semicircle on the floor. They were all kids. New hands on her shoulders forced Teresa to the floor between the semicircle and the table. Barnie was planted beside her, but communication with him was impossible.

As the figures settled in behind them, Teresa heard the rustle of collapsing skirts, the soft rasp of corduroy slacks, the crinkle of starched shirts. All her senses were picking up signals like mad. From the semicircle she smelled the scent of new clothes: Dynel, nylon, wool jersey, Dacron, combed cotton. Or am I losing my mind, Teresa wondered, feeling the girl's eyes on her: eyes like ray guns trained on her from above the table, waiting for her to settle down.

"Now then," the girl said again, dazzling the room with a smile bigger than before, "we are convening this special meeting because of the . . . appearance of the two Intruders on the floor.

"Shall we just run through the basic surveillance-and-seizure operation as we've activated it? And I'll call on the various Duty Personnel involved, beginning with Early Warning. Let's see, who was Early Warning? Oh yes, Threads." She smiled vividly out across the group, and somebody behind Teresa stood up.

The kids were all shoeless like her and Barnie, as far as she could tell. Threads turned out to be a boy. He brushed past her, heading for the table in his sock feet. The socks had a pattern of Gucci bars on them. She caught a glimpse of cream gabardine, straight-legged pleated-front slacks and another Gucci bar on the belt buckle.

The girl in charge turned her little hand in the air as a gesture of welcome, and Threads murmured, "Thank you, Madame Chairperson." He spoke in the same undertone as she had. It was like a foreign language you could understand, but you had to listen.

Threads cleared his throat, which descended in a long V down into a silky shirt with turned-back cuffs. A couple of gold chains crossed under his clavicles. Teresa figured he was good-looking. At least he had a good jaw, but the rest of his face was shadowed by the brim of a Panama straw hat with a grosgrain band. He cast a hooded glance down at her.

"Well, here's the way it went down," Threads drawled, very hang loose. "Subjects first sighted on the thirteenth at twenty-one-fifteen hundred hours, ascending escalator from main against Early Egress Traffic Pattern, fifteen minutes before Closing Time, thereby exciting suspicion.

"Subjects described as male and female, evident inner-city types, probably junior-high level or upper elementary—"

A voice somewhere behind Teresa whispered, "Some of these grade-school kids are as big as Godzilla."

"—And were tracked to Beds and Bedding, thereby exciting extreme suspicion. Both took cover at or about

102

Closing Time, just before Sweep Out. The male"—he nodded down at Barnie, who was staring up in a stupor—"took cover in the bolster of a heart-shaped Special Order." Madame Chairperson rolled her eyes to heaven. "The female, being bigger, took cover under a queen-size. Both—"

"Yes, thank you, Threads," Madame Chairperson said. "They certainly did make themselves at home, didn't they?" She waved Threads away. "That takes us through Early Warning. Who stood guard A.C.T.?"

Threads was lounging back to the semicircle. "I put Scuba on the case," he said, "and activated an All-Store Alert, naturally."

"Naturally," she said. "Scuba, where are you?"

Something rubberish brushed past Teresa, giving her the shudders. The frightful figure joined Madame Chairperson up at her command post. It was a spidery little guy in a black wet suit and flippers. Underwater goggles were perched up high on his smooth, rubber-covered head. His face was only a pale oval bordered in black.

"Thank you, Madame Chairperson," he mumbled in a somewhat sullen voice that was changing. "Subjects made no move until after the nightwatchman's rounds. At approximately twelve-forty hours, on the fourteenth of the month, they broke cover and rendezvoused. Male's voice muted but clear, saying 'One footstep could give us away,' and other unnecessary yakking. After some standing around, both subjects ascended escalator to TV and Sound Systems on eight."

103

Teresa sensed a new kind of silence behind her. This last part of the account seemed to scandalize the semicircle.

"Evidently finding the nightwatchman asleep, they descended past seven on the escalator and beyond my perimeters." Scuba fell silent and planted webby little hands on his shiny black hipbones.

"Very well, Scu—"

"All I got to say," Scuba continued in a small but penetrating voice, "is they had a whole lot more luck than they deserved—nothing but pure, dumb luck."

"All *right*, Scuba," Madame Chairperson said, sending him off. "Just the facts." Scuba walked stiffly away from the drop-leaf table, flopping his flippers before him. He angled around Barnie on his way and kicked him on the thigh, repeating, "Dumb luck."

"Where was the next sighting?" Madame Chairperson asked, lightly touching her golden crown of curls.

"Not Coeds College Bound," came a distant, level voice from the semicircle.

"I don't want to know where they weren't; I want to know where they *were*," Madame Chairperson snapped. "So shut up, Betty.

"According to my reading it was the lower level," Madame Chairperson went on. "And that would be either Julia or Rosemary."

The crowd behind Teresa and Barnie stirred. It was no more than the sound of breeze through trees. "Rosemary *was* at her post in Popular Prices, wasn't she?" Madame Chairperson inquired in a razor-sharp voice.

The breeze continued through the trees. "And by the way, where is Rosemary *now*?"

Silence.

"Or Julia?"

A voice said, "Julia's either still requisitioning or getting lunch ready."

Lunch? Teresa thought. It must be two A.M. Still—

"That girl!" Madame Chairperson stamped a little socked foot. "Betty, go into the Dining Vignette and see if Julia's in there setting the table or something. And step on it."

"Bor-ring," came Betty's voice, just slightly too faint to carry all the way up to the drop-leaf table.

Teresa huddled on the floor, staring down at Barnie's small hand gripping his knee. He didn't seem to have a plan. Above them Madame Chairperson was beginning to drum fingers on the table. Teresa's mind whirled. She caught sight of a red SOLD tag on the table. She could even read the buyer's name: Mrs. Noel Glickman, 285 Chestnut, Maplewood. Oh, Mrs. Glickman, Teresa thought, I sure wish I was at your house. I sure wish—

Something long and striped flapped past Teresa's shoulder. It was female and bigger than Teresa, almost a candidate for Tall Girls. She joined Madame Chairperson behind the table, towering over her. She wore a long chef's apron with a bib top and a big mushroom-shaped cap pulled down over one ear. She doesn't need that extra height, Teresa thought crazily. She was carrying a spatula in a large red hand, like that cook on TV.

"Look, Madame Chairperson," the cook managed to

thunder quietly, "I'm trying to get a meal on the table. I got a tray of Jell-O out there that's sweating bullets and—"

"Jell-O again," came Betty's voice from the group. "Could you puke?"

"All in good time, Julia," Madame Chairperson said, smiling, but only a little. "We're all simply famished. But first, your report."

Julia scooped a strand of hair out of her eyes with the spatula and fetched up a deep breath. "Right. Subjects sighted approximately oh-one-hundred hours on the fourteenth entering Gourmet via California Wines. Wandering in an erratic traffic pattern, they exited the department and entered upon Popular Prices where—"

"And that would be Rosemary's department," Madame Chairperson broke in.

"Forget Rosemary," Julia said. "They weren't there that long. Pantyhose inflicted superficial wounds on the female—"

Teresa's eyes bugged out, and Barnie stirred.

"—and both male and female recurred in Gourmet, heading in a direct line to deli where the female, who's a real klutz, fell down behind the counter."

Teresa's face flushed.

"Does that conclude your report?" Madame Chairperson asked.

"No. But the next part is ab-so-lutely incredible." Julia had the full attention of the room. "The two . . . subjects then proceeded to eat deli straight out of the refrigeration unit."

Betty's voice broke the horrified silence. "Gross. Fantastically gross."

"Yes, well go on, Julia. Wrap it up."

Julia shifted the bib top on her apron. "That's about it. The female eliminated, and both male and female exited via the escalator. Look, I've got corned beef, cole slaw, cucumbers in vinegar, and enough prune danishes for everybody in there in the Dining Vignette, and you know all that stuff leaves odors, and I think we ought to—"

"Yes, yes, how right you are, Julia," Madame Chairperson's sweet small voice cut in. "Thanks to our Intruders, lunch has been inexcusably delayed, which is another mark against them. I move—and second the motion—that we break for nourishment and reconvene at oh-three-hundred hours for the trial. And I won't bother to ask for a show of hands on that. Now then, who's going to stand guard over the Prisoners while we eat?"

"Scuba," Threads said.

"Scuba it is," Madame Chairperson said. Teresa could hear the whole semicircle rising to its feet behind them. Madame Chairperson, tiny and graceful, walked between Teresa and Barnie. Turning her head, Teresa saw the blazer boy step out of the crowd, followed by Threads. The three of them led the others into the room beyond the doorway.

Teresa and Barnie sat side by side, waiting. But for what? The *trial*, Teresa thought, blood pounding on her ear drums. The trial . . .

Scuba was standing over them, spidery, slick. "One word," he whispered. "I hear just . . . one . . . word, and I'll have *you* for lunch."

Teresa sagged in the shag. And so did Barnie.

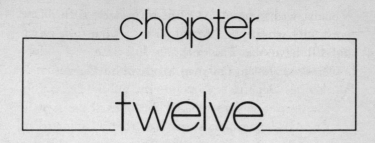

chapter

twelve

Teresa shifted just a little. Enough to see Barnie's bleached features without turning her head. They both sat there under Scuba, trying not to breathe noticeably. Finally her lips formed a word: *Trial?*

Barnie saw, she knew, though his eyes seemed fixed on the white shag. He looked very blank, but his lips formed a word too.

Mother? Teresa thought. He wants his mother? Naw, couldn't be. *Morning.* That was it. Morning? Her mind gunned in neutral, and then the wheels began to turn. Morning! Executions are held at dawn. No consolation there. But wait. If they could make it till morning store hours, this bunch of night-blooming Nazis would have to melt back into the woodwork.

Or would they? Teresa's eyes scanned the room.

What was this place? A sort of showcase for furniture in a homelike setting—vignette. That's what Julia called the dining room. This was no full-time . . . clubhouse or whatever. This was a part of the Furniture & Furnishings Department, open to the public. Decorators did these up. She remembered the ones she'd seen in Macy's. All department stores had them. Living-room vignettes. Nursery vignettes. Kitchen vignettes. All this bunch had to do was draw the drapes across these setups at night and—

The curtains rustled. Teresa never turned a hair. Do I care? she thought. I hope it's the nightwatchman. I hope it's the chief of police. I hope it's Fidel Castro.

Scuba jerked and took a step toward the curtains. More drapes, the inner ones, sighed silkily, and somebody slipped inside.

Scuba uncoiled and relaxed as much as the rubber suit allowed. ". . . Dizzy little dip," he snarled. Faint footfalls approached.

Teresa couldn't stifle a stare. This new one was . . . weirder than the others. She was about Teresa's age, but scrawnier. There was nothing much to her face but little birdlike bones. Deep purple eye shadow an inch thick covered her lids. Raven black hair, straight with floppy turnups at the end, fell to her shoulders and flowed down over her . . . costume.

It was really Early Halloween, Teresa thought. Kind of a peasant blouse with a drawstring neckline and a bodice that laced down the front. Four chiffon sashes in pastel shades trailed down over a floor-length circle skirt printed in faded palm trees and moons over the sea.

"Ohhhh," she said in a tiny voice, "the Intruders . . . captured. How romantic."

"Your tail's in a wringer, Rosemary," Scuba rasped. "You've been missed again. Madame Chairperson called for your report and—"

"Madame Chairperson?" Rosemary breathed. "You mean Barbie?"

"Yes, I mean Barbie, you brainless ding-a-ling," Scuba shrilled. "But she's Madame Chairperson to you.

"Anyway, when she called for your report, Julia tried to cover for you. But you're AWOL, and they all know it, you little—"

"AWOL?" Rosemary said in a daze.

"You know AWOL," Scuba growled. "Absent Without Leave."

"Oh, catch me lest I faint," Rosemary murmured. "And I suppose now they're all having luncheon?"

"Where else?"

"What did Julia requisition?" Rosemary inquired. She was putting Scuba off guard, Teresa could tell. Her little voice was too innocent, far more innocent than Madame—than Barbie's.

"Corned beef, Jell-O, prune danishes. A lot of good stuff, which you've missed."

"Oh, I couldn't eat a bit," Rosemary sighed. "All that reading leaves me so . . . overwrought."

"You diz—"

"But listen, Scuba, enough about me." Rosemary re-

111

arranged her sashes in a modest manner. "Why don't you go into the Dining Vignette and have a little something? You know how fast corned beef always goes. And I'll guard the Prisoners."

"You? Don't make me laugh. You couldn't—"

"It'll be like a punishment for me." Rosemary lay a hand on Scuba's rubber arm. "Like whips and chains, only more useful . . . Why should we both go hungry?"

Scuba hesitated. "I could handle them both with my bare fists, but you better have something." He looked around and then made for the fireplace where he eased a brass-handled poker out of a set of fire tools. His flippers whispered back through the shag. "Here, stand over them and keep them quiet. If they get out of line, tranquilize them with this." The poker changed hands. Then his flippers whispered away, out of the vignette.

Teresa watched Barnie's eyes follow Rosemary as she circled in on them. She held the poker with both hands in the folds of her skirt, like a golf club.

And then she bent down in an exaggerated little crouch between them and said in a breathy small voice, "Hello there."

Teresa was hypnotized by all the moons and palm trees on the skirt. She tore her eyes away and looked up beneath Rosemary's purple eyelids.

"I don't suppose anyone has thought to say welcome," Rosemary purred. "Welcome."

Teresa's jaw went slack. She chanced a glance at Barnie. He couldn't seem to take his eyes off the poker.

"Oh, it's all right to talk if you whisper so nobody but me can hear. Feel free to pour out your hearts."

Teresa caught a whiff of perfume: Devon Violets, by the smell of it. Teresa's tongue was cleaving to the roof of her mouth, but Rosemary's little beaked face was nodding encouragement. Well whatever, Teresa thought, she's not like the rest of them.

"Whips?" Teresa whispered, ". . . and chains?"

Rosemary frowned a little and put her head on one side. "Oh, that!" she whispered back. "What I said to Scuba? That's just my way of talking." She gave the poker a playful little sway. "You see, I do lots of reading. I'm such a bookworm. When I was in school—oh!"

Rosemary caught at a strand of her black hair and pulled it lightly over her nose. "We don't talk about school here." Her eyes danced all over the vignette. "But anyway, when I was . . . *there*, I was a very Gifted reader. I never knew . . . multiplication tables or any of that, but oh my, I was reading miles above my head.

"My Duty Station is Popular Prices, you know. But I'm always in the Book Department. I even go there during S.H.!"

"S?" Teresa said. "H?"

"Store Hours." Rosemary rolled her eyes dramatically. "Not like now. Now is A.C.T.: After Closing Time. I can't keep away from books. I'm a reading junkie."

"Oh."

113

"Have you read *Passion's Proudest Prize?*" Rosemary asked, flipping at the pile with the poker. "Or *This Forbidden Desire?* They're new. I'm reading them both at once."

"Haven't gotten around to them," Teresa muttered, noticing Barnie's finger tapping his temple.

"Oh, but you must!" Rosemary nudged her a little with the poker. "They're so romantic. The girls are always so . . . pure. And the men—" Rosemary drew her elbows together and closed her lids. "Oh, I can't talk about the men. They're all so marvelously . . . silent. Like your friend here.

"I only read romances," Rosemary explained. "The long ones—with canopied beds and hoofbeats pounding through the night—oh, I can't even talk about them. Have you read *The Darkness Is My Undoing?*"

"Been meaning to," Teresa mumbled. A faint odor of cucumber salad wafted in from the dining vignette.

"Do you like my outfit?" Rosemary fished up the hem of her skirt with the business end of the poker. She was wearing lace-trimmed bobby socks that had a sort of pantaloon effect. "It's Recycled Nostalgia."

"It would be," Teresa said.

"They have a new Nostalgia Boutique on six, next to Better Dresses. You'd never think all those wonderful things were secondhand and all dry-cleaned too. I'm waiting for a velvet cloak and something with just no neckline at all." She hunched up her little shoulders, and the mouth of the drawstring blouse smiled widely.

114

"Say, listen, Rosemary," Teresa began. Barnie's mouth was gaping open, but no sound was likely from there. "I wonder if you'd maybe answer a couple questions for us."

"Questions?" Rosemary's heavy hair swayed across her face. "I've always thought that Love is the Eternal Question, haven't you?"

"Ah . . . basically," Teresa said. Barnie was practically tapping a hole in his temple. "But what I mean is, it looks like we've broken a whole lot of rules that . . . you people have. And we don't even know what the rules are. It's like being in a new school. Scratch that—I didn't mean *school*. They're even going to have a trial—"

"Oh, yes." Rosemary nodded. "There's always a courtroom scene."

"But look," Teresa said, getting desperate, "we're only going to get in deeper if we don't know what's going on. Can you dig that, Rosemary?"

"Oh, utterly. Perhaps I could help you, as long as it's Our Guilty Secret." Rosemary's eyes rocketed wildly around the vignette again. "It's all terribly complicated though. We're a very highly evolved society. Otherwise we'd all be in Correctional Facilities, wouldn't we? Can't you just picture the stone walls, the drawbridge, the rats, the branding irons, the—"

"Hold it, Rosemary. Back to the rules. What is one?"

"Let me think. What's your name?"

"My name's Teresa. This here's Barnie."

"Aha!" Rosemary laughed. "You've just broken one of our bigger rules. We never give our former names. Indeed, my darling, you don't know mine. You see, that way if one of us gets . . . separated, she—or he—can't finger the rest of us. It's a very practical rule, and terribly romantic. I mean, what if you found out that Threads's - name was really *Elmer* or something? Wouldn't you just cry your eyes out?"

"Possibly," Teresa said. "Okay, so no real names."

"Oh, but what we call ourselves here *are* our real names now." Rosemary wrinkled her bird brow. "This *is* our reality.

"I mean we can be *anything* we want to be, as long as Barb—as long as we conform to the group. It's really a lot like sch—other situations. Take Scuba for example—"

"You take Scuba," Teresa muttered. "You can handle him. Seems like some kind of a sadist to me."

"Oh, do you think so?" Rosemary's eyes expanded until there was hardly any purple showing. "I always thought of a sadist as a much older man, with a mustache, riding a horse, with no shirt on."

Rosemary was momentarily lost in thought or something. Barnie shook his head hopelessly.

"But anyway," she went on suddenly, "Scuba's called Scuba because his Duty Station's Aquatic Equipment, on three, and—"

"Hold it . . . Rosemary," Teresa said. "I'm trying to follow you, but I'm falling behind."

"Oh! Well, you know, we all have our Duty Sta-

116

tions: store departments we're assigned to for NP—Night Patrol and OSHS—Occasional Store Hours Surveillance. Everybody except Barbie. Barbie can do anything she wants to."

Barnie gave Teresa a knowing look, the first one of their captivity.

"But when Barbie was younger," Rosemary continued, "she was assigned to Toys, on five. But Dolly's there now. Of course we can't just hang out in our departments all the time. But we're there quite a lot. We know how to blend in so the clerks don't really notice us.

"Scuba's assigned to Aquatic Equipment. You know Aquatic Equipment?"

"Surfboards," Barnie said, picking at the shag, "like that."

"Yes," Rosemary said, smiling fondly at him. "Like that. So Scuba wears that little wet suit and goggles, and sometimes he carries the darlingest little transistorized harpoon."

Rosemary gave the carpet several pokes with the poker. The price tag on it flickered like a moth. "And Threads is assigned the Mod Shop, and Julia's in Gourmet, and Ken's in the Varsity Shop, and Betty's in—"

"Coeds College Bound," Teresa said, remembering.

"Oh, you're very quick!" Rosemary smiled. "Of course poor me! I should be assigned either to the Nostalgia Boutique or the Book Department. They're sort of my Body and Soul. But they're too small. The departments, I mean. So they assigned me Popular Prices. The lower-

117

class stores would call it Bargain Basement. Popular Prices isn't really *me,* but I don't mind.

"I mean, what kind of a group would we be without one misfit?" Rosemary smiled somewhat madly and seemed to spell out several words on the carpet with the poker.

"I dress way down when I'm on duty," she explained, "except I often forget when I *am* on duty. Why, I'm almost never there, aren't I awful? The Popular Prices clerks wouldn't know me from Dame Barbara Cartland. The only time one of them tried to wait on me was when I got carried away and was reading the pantyhose packages!" She laughed helplessly, and purple tears rolled down her cheeks.

"I read anything because I'm so Gifted. Of course *all* the kids here *say* they're Gifted, even Dolly. But I really am. So I simply read and read. But it's those romance books that just carry me away on lovely soft wings. Besides, I have such a good friend in the Book Department—"

"Who's that?" Teresa inquired, wondering who'd be a match for Rosemary.

Rosemary's purple lids lowered. "Did I say that? I mean the books *themselves* are my best friends. But what I was going to explain is that we're supposed to match our departments, in case we have to freeze."

"Freeze?" A chill invaded Teresa.

"Yes. You know—" Rosemary jerked once, and her eyes snapped into a fixed glaze. One of her hands stopped in the air and seemed to turn to plaster. The poker stopped poking. Rosemary froze into a dress dummy.

"Oh," Teresa said. "Freeze. I'm beginning to get the picture."

"Isn't it droll?" Rosemary moved and broke her spell. "Once I stood absolutely unmoving for three hours in a Popularly Priced display of real dummies for 'Back to Sch—' I mean, Fall Fashions."

"Far out," Teresa said. "But what about somebody like Julia? Gourmet doesn't have dummies."

"Too true," Rosemary replied, "and besides, Julia sweats. Mostly she just has to take cover during the day, though once when the woman who demonstrates those cute little kitchen knives didn't show up, Julia took her place. She made over four hundred radish rosettes that day and sold quite a lot of knives."

"Really far out," Teresa breathed.

"Really," said Rosemary.

"But you don't mean to tell me Scuba stalks around Aquatic Equipment during Store Hours in that rig of his."

"Oh, not often," Rosemary said, vaguer now. "Mostly at night. A.C.T., I mean. For Night Patrol."

"But what's the point? There aren't any Store Personnel or customers around—A.C.T."

"There are . . . other problems." Rosemary shuddered.

Barnie's head was in his two hands like it was pounding.

Teresa knew the feeling. "So let me get this straight,

Rosemary. Sometimes you're all just kids roaming around the store like customers. Sometimes you impersonate dress dummies. Sometimes at night—A.C.T.—you're up here in your vignette. Sometimes you take cover and sleep. And sometimes you're pulling guard duty."

Rosemary sighed. "You've really captured the *rhythm* of our life. Except you've left out that we have an awful lot of meetings. Barbie likes them. But you really *understand*. It's too bad—"

Teresa didn't want to hear whatever was coming next. "I guess you really got to be on your toes to keep ahead of the nightwatchman—"

"Oh, yes."

"And that plainclotheswoman, Bertha—"

"Bertha, the Booster-Basher?"

"Bertha who?" Teresa asked.

"Bertha handles the shoplifters, who are known in the trade as *boosters*. Bertha bashes them. But she never even notices us. We never boost anything much, certainly never during Store Hours."

"Ah . . . right, Rosemary. So the adults around here don't give you any big hassles."

"Adults?" Rosemary said. "You just use a little common sense around them. How much does it take to keep ahead of adults? *We're* Gifted. Who ever heard of a Gifted grown-up? I'd hate to think what would happen to this store if it was left to *adults*. Why, they're not even here most of the time. No. We have other enemies—"

Rosemary's grip tightened on the poker. Her dreamy eyes vanished beneath their purple burden. She drew back from Teresa.

And Teresa drew forward a little, trying to keep her talking. "Well, scratch that too, Rosemary. But listen, where did all you people come from?"

Rosemary's lids flew upon in real horror. "Oh never, never ask that!" she whispered. "That's worse than mentioning sch—you know, that place with blackboards."

"Well, shoot, Rosemary. How are Barn . . . this guy here and I ever going to learn anything unless we ask?"

"Don't ask anybody else if you know what's good for you. Besides, you can see for yourself that everybody probably came from a very good family background. I don't suppose there's anybody here who didn't have color TV in their own room. But you know what a drag families can be, all those rules they lay on you."

"More rules than around here?" Teresa asked.

"Well, that's different . . . I think. But never mind about that. I'll just tell you a little tiny part of my own history—what I don't mind telling—but that's all. I mean I'm such a misfit, anything goes with me; only don't tell the others.

"You see I was shopping with my grandmother. And

she had a stroke or something right here in Paradise Park. It was in Discount-o-Rama, which is sort of embarrassing. But I just walked away and found myself in Forbes and Ledsmar."

"When was that?"

Rosemary went vague again. "Oh, time doesn't mean anything to me. It was the year *Sweet Madness of the Heart* was published. In paperback." She drifted away then, murmuring, "I can't say any more. Besides the others are coming back. Be quiet now." She ground the poker point deep into the shag. "Be just as quiet as little mice."

The others were coming back all right. Teresa sensed them, but it was the most orderly mass movement of kids she'd ever experienced. She tried to be sitting exactly as she had been before.

The blazer boy—Ken—led Barbie up to the drop-leaf table, bowed just slightly to her smile, and dissolved back into the semicircle.

Barbie nudged her blousy sleeves back from her porcelain wrists and smiled again out over the group. Then she skimmed Barnie and Teresa with a glittering glance, pursed her Cupid's-bow lips, and said, "Court has now reconvened. I have only one opening remark. I find the Criminals before us already Guilty."

chapter

thirteen

A decorator bronze refrigerator/freezer had recently been uncrated in the Contemporary Kitchen vignette. It stood beside a laminated wood chopping block. The crate it came in was wedged back between a microwave oven and a stainless-steel countertop. On the countertop stood a kitchen-match holder in the shape of a chicken. The crate spoke in two voices.

"Every time I make a move, I get a splinter right up my—" said Barnie's voice.

"So don't move. Every time you do, you're all over me. It's like being collared by Bertha the Booster-Basher," said Teresa.

"We ought to have luck like that. Bertha's only half-crazy."

"I'm going to be all the way crazy if you don't stop shifting around."

"Well, I can't sit, and I can't stand, and if I could just get my—"

"That's not yours. It's mine."

"Oh, sorry."

"Sorry's the word. This thing they put us in makes under the queen-size seem like the World Trade Center."

"Yeah. Remember the old queen-size?"

"You want me to light a match? Because I could if I managed to reach down in my sock."

"A match in your sock?"

"I grabbed a handful out of that chicken thing when they were cramming us into this box. Who knows, maybe—"

"Maybe nothing. There's not enough oxygen in here to breathe. Forget matches."

Silence then for several minutes.

"Barnie?"

"I'm right here, under your chin. Where else?"

"You think the jury's still out?" Teresa tried to keep the sob out of her voice. But it was there.

"Yeah," he said. "They are, and we aren't. Some trial."

"Barnie, you didn't make things any better by demanding a lawyer."

"How was I supposed to know I'd get Julia? She was prejudiced against me from the start."

"Anyway, we learned something. They never eat anything out of Gourmet because it might be missed. They stick strictly to Employees' Cafeteria leftovers, which nobody'd miss. What's *requisition* mean, by the way?"

"Steal," Barnie said.

"I figured it was in that general area."

"I got to hand it to you, Teresa, acting in your own defense. I think they admired you for trying."

"I was afraid they'd give me Rosemary."

"Chees," Barnie said. "You were pretty wise when they asked you your name and you said, 'Teresa because it isn't.'"

"And you picked right up on it and played along. If we got to go, Barnie, at least we're going to go togeth—"

"You figured out who they think we are, Teresa? You heard Rosemary. She was about to spill her guts before the trial. These people have got enemies. You think they figure we're from the enemy side?"

"Who knows?" she said. "The jury's still out. And since we already know we're guilty of something or other, what's the sentence going to be? These people don't seem the abolish-capital-punishment type to me. We could end up at the bottom of an elevator shaft like chopped liver."

"Or it could be just plain slow starvation in this box," Barnie said. "I'm already slowly starving." Hands gripped the crate, crashing Teresa and Barnie against the side. They slipped down till their knees jammed together. Fresher air whisked in from the open bottom.

"All right, you two, start crawling out," Scuba's voice said hollowly, "or I'll come in there and—"

"Okay, okay, we're coming," Teresa said. "See? We're crawling backward. Get off my hand, Barnie."

A quick march later they stumbled back into the living-room vignette. The jury, which was everybody, sat on the floor. One muscular goon in a sweat shirt labeled "Butch" looked up at Teresa, lolled his tongue out of his mouth, and gave her the thumbs-down sign. Thanks a lot, creep, Teresa thought.

Madame Chairperson—Barbie—stood at the drop-leaf table between Threads and Ken. They looked like an advertisement for a modeling school. Barbie gave everybody a fond, welcoming smile and remarked, "Prisoners to their knees." Teresa and Barnie crumpled under Scuba's hands.

Barbie made a little throat-clearing sound and said, "I'll just begin the Trial with a few tiny comments since we don't have all night. Unless you two fellows have anything to say?"

Barbie divided a coy look between Ken and Threads. They looked daggers at each other.

"In that case, I repeat, I find the Prisoners before us: 'Teresa' and 'Barnie'—haven't they picked precious names? Too inner city! Anyway, I find them guilty of Intruding on Our Turf, Committing Independent Acts, Endangering Our Cover with an Eye Toward Blowing It, Eating Unauthorized Foodstuffs, and in the case of the female, Changing Clothes Without Permission."

The crowd murmured, and Barbie's voice fell to new dramatic lows. "As we know, these are all felonies, aren't they?"

The crowd quietly hissed, "Yes."

"But," Barbie went on, "I find the Intruders possibly guilty of something a whole lot nastier. I suspect 'Teresa' and 'Barnie' are Spies."

"Spies," the crowd hissed almost silently.

"Yes, Spies, sent to infiltrate us from the enemy side. In short"—Barbie drew herself up—"if you ask me, I say they're a couple of Mouth-Breathers."

The jury sat in troubled silence. "What are Mouth-Breathers?" Teresa asked.

"Shut up," Barbie replied and then managed a small smile. "I call now for the jury's decision, and it better be the right one. Who's the Foreperson?"

Somebody stirred behind Teresa. "Is it you, Betty? Well, come up and take the floor—for a minute."

Teresa fought a new wave of hysteria by concentrating on Betty, who'd only been a voice before. A pair of ribbed knee socks swept past her, and Betty rounded the table into the glow surrounding Madame Chairperson.

Betty looked older than the rest: a haggard fifteen at least. Her mouth was a thin line, and her hair was drawn straight back and skewered with a barrette. But it was her outfit that really put the years on her. It was pure Coeds College Bound: a fawn-colored gored skirt under a green-flecked tweed jacket over a mustard suede vest. Chic, but severe, Teresa judged, seeming to go down for the third time under waves of insanity.

Betty planted a hand near the small of her back and almost won a staring contest with Barbie. "Welllll,

Madame Chairperson," she said at last in a grim little buzz-saw voice, "as we all know, hung juries are bor-ring.

"Nevertheless the jury members really can't get their act together on the Mouth-Breather charge, which is of course the Big Number. I mean we've——"

"For Pete's sake," Teresa interrupted, "what's a Mouth-Breather?"

"One more outburst from the female prisoner, and she goes back in the crate," Barbie said in a sweet voice. "And from you, Betty, I want a verdict, not a ninety-minute Dinah Shore talk show."

Betty's eyes snapped, but she only said, "Guilty on all those lesser counts, which are bor-ring. Proved neither Guilty nor Not Guilty as Mouth-Breathers."

Betty held her ground while Barbie smoldered. "Well, I've heard of sloppy jury work before," she spat, "but this about takes the bagel. Those other charges don't mean squat without a——"

"Listen, Barb—Madame Chairperson," Betty barked, "I was President of the entire Student Council at my school and——"

"At your *what*, Betty?" Barbie smiled poisonously. "Maybe you'd care to tell us all about your . . . *school* and your entire family background, which was probably terribly, terribly top-drawer. Anybody who'd mention school would probably even mention *parents*. Possibly you'd even like to tell us your former name, which was no doubt prominent. I'm sure it'd make quite a pretty little story, and then we'd all have the goods on you for any future . . . use."

Betty began to fold. She shrank, un-Sanforized, inside the Harris tweed and suede. Her hand faltered down. She slunk back to the semicircle. "Could you simply puke?" she whispered in a broken voice.

"Sergeants-at-arms?" Barbie flashed smiles all over Ken and Threads. "Would you please seize the Prisoners and put them on their feet for the Sentencing?" Barbie bobbed her head in controlled excitement. Ken and Threads were behind Barnie and Teresa. Threads had Teresa's armpits in a vise. Barnie seemed to hang suspended in the air before Ken. "This is the part I really like," Barbie said.

She milked the moment for all it was worth. Her little hand perked up the bow at her neck and wandered over her golden curls.

She was just opening her mouth to speak when drapery hooks squealed along a curtain rod. The inner drapes twitched, bulged, and flapped open. A boy staggered through.

"It's Swank," somebody said, "from Cuff Links and Body Jewelry."

Whoever he is, Teresa thought, he's in terrible shape. Somebody had blacked both his eyes. They were swelling already. And some deadly weapon had creased his face from forehead to chin. The wound looked like red HO-gauge railroad tracks. Dark blood edged a split lip. One of his ears looked unnaturally bent and seemed to be changing shape.

"How sick-making!" Betty's voice said.

As crowds do, the group drew back from Swank

instead of rushing forward. He swayed a moment, and then managed to say, "Mouth-Breathers. The place is crawling with them." Then he crumpled in a heap on the white shag.

Barbie turned a terrible color. "This is just what I've always tried to avoid. A direct confrontation."

"Count me out," Threads said from far beneath his hat brim. "What if they tore my shirt? It's real silk. I could never get it back into stock."

The semicircle broke into a seething mass, milling and flapping like disturbed doves. A table lamp went over.

"Battle stations, everybody!" Barbie cried softly, all her smiles blurring. Someone doused the lights, and from where she still stood to be sentenced, Teresa was jostled and elbowed by unseen forms. Gray light appeared as someone yanked back the drapes and the forms poured out.

"Be still, my heart!" Rosemary said softly. She was the last to leave, judging from the lingering scent of Devon Violets. "This could be a *very* Unhappy Ending."

chapter

fourteen

Teresa reached for Barnie in the blacked-out vignette. "Barn?" He wasn't where he'd been.

"Close the drapes," he said. "I'm crawling toward the lamp."

She stood up and teetered in the darkness, took one step and fell over something. I'm always doing this, she thought, feeling carpeting in her nose. She planted a hand to raise herself up, and it closed over another hand, bigger, covered with rings.

"Holy—" She remembered then that it must be Swank. She rolled herself off his body and stood up. With outstretched hands she walked to where the drapes should be. Fiberglas, she thought, getting a handful and pulling the curtain across slowly so the hooks wouldn't squeak.

131

The lamp went on. Barnie was staring across the vignette at her, somewhat wild eyed. Well, it's been a rough night, Teresa thought. Between them Swank lay cradled in carpeting, looking terminal. They crept together, meeting over Swank's form.

"You want to cut out?" Teresa said, "because if this" —she pointed down to the motionless figure—"is the only thing between us and freedom, I don't think we've got a worry in the world."

"You kidding?" Barnie said. "They're having World War Three all over the store, and you think we can just shag on out of here?"

"Worth a shot," Teresa said. "Give me a chance and I'd walk all the way back to town. After this, Harley Probst and his Kobras wouldn't mean diddle to me."

"They would when you got there," Barnie muttered.

Swank writhed slightly and tried to open swollen eyes. Teresa had no idea what he looked like beneath the wounds. Barnie squatted on his heels.

Swank tried to focus on him. "Mouth-Breather?"

"Naw," Barnie said. "Don't worry about us. We're just a—couple of newcomers."

"Need all the help we can get," Swank said, turning ashier. "They're taken Active Sportswear and Men's Toiletries as far as Aramis. They didn't penetrate from the parking-lot entrance, but they've got those doors open now somehow."

"Listen," Teresa said, "forget about that. You need a doctor."

Swank's wounds burned a brighter pink. "You kidding? My *father's* a doctor. None of those turkeys have made a house call since the Korean War, and there's a six-week wait for office visits. And without Blue Cross, and I'm talking Major Medical—"

"Okay, okay," she said. He must be in bad shape if he's running his mouth about Family Background, she thought. "What'd they slam you with across the face?" She reached out and just touched his nose, which seemed to be mainly intact.

"The usual," Swank murmured. "Bicycle chains. I got an antenna on the ear too. Is it swelling bad?"

"It's a little bigger than the other one," Barnie said.

"And you can imagine how much of a dent I could make with nothing but a gold-plated watch chain and a handful of astrological bangles. I broke a long-handled shoehorn over one of their heads, but she just kept coming on."

"How many of them are there?" Teresa sensed that all escape was cut off.

"Who knows? Their whole strike force. It's like being blitzed by an entire Remedial Reading class." Swank's tongue came out to explore the split lip and retreated.

"And you stood the whole bunch off alone?"

"You nuts? I'd be in the trunk of a Cougar now if our Night Patrol shift hadn't been on duty."

"You mean," Barnie said, "there are more of you— I mean us?"

"Sure," Swank said, easing a ringed hand up to his ear, "two full shifts. You really are newcomers, aren't

133

you?" Teresa and Barnie shrank. "Oh, I can see now you're not Mouth-Breathers. Where you from, the city?"

"How'd you know?" Teresa said, looking down at her new outfit again: the absolutely fresh shirt and sweater coordination.

"You've got the basic, all-over look," Swank said. "Listen, I know you may be feeling neutral, but our side could use all the muscle they can get. We're more Gifted than they are, brain-wise, but one-on-one . . ."

In another minute Teresa and Barnie were out at the escalator. There was the muffled rustle of armies clashing by night seven floors below. And the nearer noise of a late-late-late movie from the Sony up on eight. "Some nightwatchman," Barnie said, shaking his head. "And he gets a salary for that?"

They started down into the darkness, heading for the front lines.

"I don't know about this," Teresa said as they rounded the Bath Shop and Toys on five. "As I see it, either way we lose. The Store People win, and we get sentenced. The Mouth-Breathers win, and we get creamed. Who are these Mouth-Breathers anyway?"

"I got my ideas," Barnie said, creeping lower. "My hunch is they're a bunch of suburban greaseballs, and the parking lot's their turf. And what they'd like is a piece of the in-store action. When you think about it, life's pretty soft in here. What have they got going out there? Sleep in a pile of radial tires or on sacks of

Weed 'N' Feed. Probably even have to go home at night, if they have homes."

"I wish they'd gone home tonight. But either way they don't sound like the type to get allowances. What do you figure they live off of?"

"What did Harley Probst and the Kobras live off of? Hubcaps, CB radios, ripped-off tape decks, chrome stripping, Mercedes hood ornaments. The pickings in a parking lot aren't slim, but still . . ."

"If the parking lot's theirs," Teresa said, "how'd we get past them when we first came?"

"They're probably too dumb to post guards." Barnie receded down to Silver Patterns and Bridal Registry on three.

Teresa was thinking like crazy, tripping down from tread to tread. "But they've got no business in this store. They're just a pack of animals. They got no organization. They'd spoil a good thing for themselves."

"Teresa," Barnie said, pausing on two, "I think you've just taken sides."

They edged down until their heads were level with the ceiling of main. The store stretched out below them. Against the dawn light filtering from the parking-lot entrance, Teresa saw figures struggling in silhouette. A barricade of Shoe Department chairs was raised this side of Active Sportswear. Arpège hung heavy all the way to the ceiling. Somebody who may have gotten an eyeful of spray cologne was writhing on the floor, fists jammed into face.

They fought in silence, though growls and snufflings came from the Mouth-Breathers. Even when the store people fell, they sank in silence. But something that could have been Julia's spatula clattered down on a far-off glass counter.

You couldn't really make out who anybody was, Teresa thought, except it was clearly Ken making a run from Personalized Stationery & Greeting Cards, carrying what looked like a desk blotter heaped with paperweights. Somebody who could have been Betty grabbed a couple from him and charged off toward Handbags & Totes. Huddled at the top of the escalator next to Barnie, Teresa tried to make some sense out of the scene.

She was barely aware of the figure approaching her from behind until a foot touched her lower back. Teresa nearly plunged all the way down to the battlefield. "Holy—"

Barnie grabbed her, and they spun around to see a skinny girl looming over them like a telegraph pole. She was ghostly pale. The small black circle of her mouth opened. "I'm Crystal, from Stemware. How's it going down there?"

"We're falling back," Barnie said. "They're swarming in here like a January White Sale."

"Oh, no," Crystal whispered. "They've taken Breakfast Sets and Bone China up here. And I don't think Collectors' Tea Cups can hold out much longer. Oh, I don't know what to do!" Crystal wrung her hands. "I hate to use the Steuben Glass on them. It's heavy, but it's so expensive. Even a minor piece retails at . . ." Crystal turned in confusion and blundered back into the darkness of the second floor.

"It looks like we've had it," Barnie said. "I wonder if the Mouth-Breathers take prisoners?"

Teresa's hand was moving down to her sock. "Swap places with me," she muttered to Barnie.

"What?"

"Move your—"

"Okay. Now you slide over. What's the idea?"

Teresa stood up. Thirty feet below her the lipstick carpet was littered with rhinestones, picking up the first rays of the sun. She gazed along the ceiling. "Get a hold on me, Barnie. I got to lean out. No, my waist, not my skirt. It'll come off in your hand. Ease me out."

She planted a sock foot on the rubber banister. "I hope these matches aren't damp. I been sweating like a pig." She scraped a match across the ceiling. On the third scratch, it flared, sending out a patch of yellow light. A nozzle on the sprinkler system cast a small, jagged shadow. "A tad farther out, Barnie," she said, never chancing a look back, or down.

She got the dwindling flame directly under the sprinkler spigot at last. The match flickered down near her thumb and finger. She felt blisters form, and her eyes watered.

A seal popped at the tip of the spigot. It spat a drop of water on the blue dot of flame as Teresa began to smell her own burning flesh. Pipes in the ceiling shuddered, then belched, then roared. A fine mist dropped in a hundred cone shapes from all over the ceiling above main.

A mist, then a drizzle, then a summer shower. Sunlight out of the parking lot cast rainbows over Body Jewelry and Jockey shorts in Hawaiian Hues. In the dimmer distance over Active Sportswear a steady rain fell on Lacoste shirts, athletic socks, and greasy Mouth-Breather heads.

Through the healing rain the lipstick-pink carpet seemed a garden path of weathered brick, dotted with jewellike wild flowers fresh with the dawn.

Teresa watched two tangling figures by the Pick Up Your Poodle sign at the foot of the escalator. It was Barbie in hand-to-hand combat with a—it was the praying-mantis girl from the parking lot. She recognized the elastic top, the cutoffs, hanging now in new tatters. And the headphones. That's a modified CB radio, she thought. The bug girl's the nerve center for the entire Mouth-Breather force.

Barbie had the big bug girl off her skateboard. It hadn't been much use on the carpeting, and it was turned wheels up against an Estée Lauder display. But Barbie was falling back, still a game little slugger. And neat. Her sleeves were pushed up on her elbows, and the bow under her chin was only a little out of line. She was landing one after another on the bug girl's chin and then making openhanded grabs for the earphones.

But the bug girl was coming on like a Pittsburgh

Steeler, taking all Barbie's punishment on the chin and handing it back with interest. Barbie danced free of most of the bigger punches, but she was retreating up the escalator now, skidding around on about the fourth wet tread.

Between two spigots near the top Teresa and Barnie had the only dry seat in the house. "What—" Barnie began.

"Just wait," Teresa told him. "You'll see."

The rain whipped up into a downpour. Teresa couldn't see past Monogramming While You Wait. And somewhere far out in the mall the sprinkler system tripped a fire alarm.

"Now watch," Teresa said, "and we'll see who keeps their heads and who doesn't."

The combatants ceased battle all over the store. There was a moment when everybody on both sides froze, in any old position. The day broke brighter over the darkening carpet. A light bulb in Perfumes blew out with a thump.

And out in the mall steel-heeled boots, running, rang out. Keys clattered against the mall entrance doors. Deep, authority-figure voices echoed over mall tile. The automatic doors were jammed. The grunts of grown-ups filtered in under the hiss of the rain as wedged doors held firm against crowbars.

The praying-mantis girl was fishing down into her elastic front and yanking up some kind of little walkie-talkie microphone, but she was spluttering into it.

Barbie dealt her a final slam that laid the mike over the bug girl's nose and sent her skidding across the floor at the foot of the escalator.

The Mouth-Breathers were ganging toward the parking-lot doors. Pitiless day played all over congealing heads, soaking cigarette packs in T-shirt sleeves, Levi's weighty with water, and sagging black leather. Down the Up escalator opposite, Teresa and Barnie watched a formation of Mouth-Breathers in flight from Bone China on two. Sunlight struck suddenly upon their studs and pierced ears.

Teresa watched them fanning out into the lot, but then they halted, looking for leadership and shelter. The praying-mantis girl scooped up her skateboard from the blotchy rug and sprinted off behind her troops.

Barbie was stumbling up the escalator, hand over hand. Midway up, she turned, damp but undamaged, and cast a strange, knowing look at Teresa and Barnie. Then, fetching up a deep breath with a sob in it, she flew past them, up to Junior Miss.

"She'll freeze up there," Teresa said.

"It's not that cold—"

"I mean *freeze.*"

"Oh." He nodded. "Like that."

Ken bounded up next, two treads at a time. Smelling strongly of wet flannel, he cocked a suave eyebrow at them and climbed on, heading for the Varsity Shop. Somehow he managed not to appear in a hurry. Cool now, and about to freeze.

Down on main Betty had frozen in a sophisticated

pose on a small platform where a dress dummy in Summer Cottons had crashed over in the aisle. "She's a mile from Coeds College Bound," Teresa said, "but she'll make that work all right."

Betty had frozen as if holding the leash of an invisible dog. Her eyes glazed beneath fringed lashes. Her gored skirt swayed into motionlessness. And the small line of her mouth was clearly not real.

The last of the survivors were reaching the escalator now. An odd couple darted down the Down into the lower level. It was Rosemary in a whirl of chiffon scarves, half-carrying Julia, who was half-strangled by apron straps. They vanished toward the distant wink of California Wines.

Threads pounded up, heading wherever the Mod Shop was. He vaulted over Teresa and Barnie, muttering, "Not a scratch on me. They didn't lay a finger on me."

"He didn't get close enough for that," Barnie remarked.

The only movement on main came from the last of the Mouth-Breathers, clawing at each other to get through to the parking lot before the cops could overtake them. A fist fight broke out between two Mouth-Breathers. A fan belt whipcracked in the air. A sand-filled ashtray went over with a cymbal crash. A female Mouth-Breather swept up three shoulder-strap handbags on her way to deliverance.

"Vinyl," Teresa said. "They keep the real leather out of reach."

141

The store was all but empty now except for the recumbent figure who'd been Arpèged. The casualty wore motorcycle boots with spurs.

"Mouth-Breather," Barnie said. It seemed a long time since he'd seen anybody wearing footgear.

From the mall entrance glass exploded over the steady clang of the fire alarm. Red rays brighter than the sun played in from a fire truck outside the parking-lot entrance. Sirens screamed indoors and out. Firemen were crisscrossing the blacktop with hoses. A cherry picker slanted into the sun, and security guards poured in through the shattered mall doors.

"Got them coming and going," Teresa said, looking down as if from heaven. "Now we pull back."

"Back to the queen-size," Barnie said.

Teresa considered. "In this outfit I could probably freeze in Junior Miss." She cradled her chin as the first fireman's ax splintered the only closed parking-lot door. "But I'll stick with you, Barn. It'll be nice to be back under the old queen-size. Probably even dry. And when they want us, they know where to find us."

chapter

fifteen

They were both still noses-to-innerspring by midmorning. Teresa had even dozed a little, off and on. It was dry under the queen-size though elsewhere in Beds & Bedding some of the sprinklers had clearly cut loose.

Some time after daybreak firemen's boots had thundered near their ears. Somebody who barked like a fire chief had sat down on the heart-shaped bed nearby. Then there'd been a loud hissing sound, confusing shouts, and bad language. Barnie'd even ventured a peek out from under the bedspread until Teresa hauled on his arm.

The firemen lumbered away. "What was that hissing all about?" Teresa whispered. "Not that cat again?"

"Naw," Barnie murmured. "The fire chief flopped down on that black heart-shaped bed to make notes or something. He had one of those foam fire extinguishers in a holster on his belt. I guess when he sat down, the extinguisher triggered and spread foam all over the bed. You talk about a mess."

"Chees," Teresa whispered. "Between the Mouth-Breathers and the firemen, this place is going to be a total ruin."

"Would that be all bad?" Barnie asked.

They dozed again before the sales personnel came in, but that bunch only wandered around awhile before being sent down to main.

Teresa was wide awake again, her fingers laced behind her head. "Hey, Barnie?"

"Yeah."

"You figure the store's closed?"

"Yeah."

"For how long?"

"Do I know? Not too long probably, though you really did a job on main, Teresa."

"Well, it worked, didn't it? We'd all be in the trunks of Cougars now if somebody hadn't broken up that battle. Those Mouth-Breathers come on like the cast of *The Warriors*."

Barnie seemed to nod.

"You think if the cops rounded them up, they'll rat on us—on the Store People, I mean?"

"Use your head," Barnie said. "What if *you* were a Mouth-Breather and tried to tell a juvenile court judge you'd been rumbling with a bunch of kids who actually *live* in the store? He'd have you in a rubber room."

Teresa gave this thought. "Good point. No adult could handle that, especially a judge. He'd just figure they got to fighting among themselves while they were ripping off the store." Teresa sighed with temporary satisfaction. "Where do you suppose the rest of *us* are?"

"Taken cover," Barnie said. "They've all got their places."

"And I know what they're all thinking right about now, too. Especially Barbie."

"About our sentence? They've got to know we're not Mouth-Breathers now. I mean if we were, you wouldn't have set off the sprinklers. The Mouth-Breathers were winning."

"Nothing wrong with your logic, Barnie. But is it Barbie's? Because I don't think so. She's out to zap us, especially me."

"How do you know?"

"A woman knows these things, Barnie. Trust me."

They lay there beneath the queen-size while the fire-fighters' foam ate deeper into the Special Order across the aisle with a faint bubbling sound.

"You think it's about evening yet, Barnie?" Teresa said finally.

"It's not even noon yet."

Teresa shifted stiffly. "It's not viable, Barn. I can't lounge around under this thing all day waiting for

Barbie's ax to fall tonight. It'll kill me. The waiting, I mean."

"I'm not exactly looking forward to it myself," Barnie said.

"You know," Teresa murmured, "the thing about Barbie is this: everybody just goes along with her because it's easier than thinking for himself."

"Also they're scared of her," Barnie pointed out.

"It's the same thing. They're scared to think for themselves. They got no street smarts, Barnie, no *grit*. They're suburban cream puffs. Like a bunch of people who want their mommies. And Barbie *is* their mommy."

"Then I'm glad I never had one," Barnie said sincerely.

"And you want to know something else, Barnie? We're beginning to think like the rest of them, like Threads and Ken and Betty and Rosemary—"

"Nobody thinks like Rosemary."

"Forget Rosemary then. You know what I'm saying. We're not going to lick Barbie on her own terms. We've got to *bring her down*. On *our* terms."

Barnie burrowed there, bunched in his lumber jacket, trying to picture Barbie brought down. "Sounds good," he said, "but—"

"But nothing. We've got to go into action while the rest of them are taking cover for the day. They're prisoners of their own routine. Every day's got to be the same with them, like school. Now you take today. The store's closed, but it's full of personnel, so they figure they can't

146

circulate. They're holed up all over the store like the Living Dead."

"So are we."

"Yeah, Barnie. But not for long. I got an idea. It's a long shot, but it might just work. Just listen a minute, and you might as well get your boots on. You and I have places to go."

The coast was clear as they made their way carefully out of Beds & Bedding. Heavy industrial fans were drying the rugs over in the Carpet Department, which smelled like a wet dog.

The escalators were empty as far down as they could see. They split up on two. Barnie raised a small hand in farewell and seemed to vanish down the escalator. Teresa turned in the direction of the Stemware Department.

Crystal was nowhere to be seen, of course, but the department was being manned by a familiar figure. It was the merchandising trainee in the Jaws II T-shirt, who was working her second day at Forbes & Ledsmar. Teresa drew nearer.

The trainee's tie-dyed skirt clung wetly to her hips. Sweaty crescent moons loomed in the underarm regions of her Jaws II T-shirt. The store's damp climate had kinked the hair that escaped from her bandanna. Teresa crept nearer, noticing that the trainee was talking to herself.

"For *this*," she was saying, "I went four years to college." She poured sprinkler water out of martini glasses into a plastic bucket.

"For *this*," she went on, "I took a Business Administration B.S. degree. B.S.," she repeated. "Believe it." She picked a glittering sliver of glass out of the toe of her wedgie and took up a cloth to dry a large display of Bohemian glass ashtrays.

"For *this*," she added, "I majored in Retailing Dynamics." She snatched down an ice bucket teetering on a shelf edge, realizing too late that it was brimful of water like everything else. It doused her. A faded shark flattened itself darkly across her front. "Do I need a job like this?" she asked the world.

"Beats me," Teresa said. "Do you?"

The merchandising trainee spun around to find Teresa standing there next to a wet wet bar, one elbow propped against a row of crystal cordials. She squinted at the intruder, taking note of her dry outfit. "Store's not open yet," the trainee said.

"Tell me something I don't know," Teresa replied.

"You work here?"

"I put in my time," Teresa said.

The merchandising trainee squinted through beaded lashes. "Say listen, I see you someplace before?"

"If you can remember as far back as yesterday," Teresa said. "The trainee session. That orientation number."

"You a trainee?" said the trainee.

Teresa, who was already standing as tall as possible, gave her a level stare.

148

"Yeah, I guess you were in that bunch," the trainee said. "Somehow, though, I didn't remember anybody as young-looking as you."

"Around here you can be as young as you want to," Teresa said, "if your uncle's the store president." This is not an outright lie, Teresa thought.

The trainee swallowed and dried a shot glass busily. "So that makes you a Forbes?" she said, deeply awed. "Or a Ledsmar maybe?"

"You can call me Teresa. What's your name?"

"Dawn Botts."

Teresa stared but took note of the name. "Up in the Executive Suite they thought I might be able to give you a hand." Now this *was* an outright lie, Teresa thought, but still—

"They did?" said Dawn Botts. "That's sort of nice of your uncle—I guess. Frankly . . . Miss—Teresa, I always thought of company presidents as Imperialist Pigs —Fawning Fascists—Republicans even. You know where I'm coming from?"

"Oh, yes." Teresa nodded. "I know exactly where you're coming from, Dawn. How about knocking off for some lunch. They'll work your tail off around here if you don't stand up for your rights. And you lead the way to the Employees' Cafeteria, Dawn. Because, frankly, I'm starved."

A hard core of four stock boys, mostly elderly, were hiding from mop-up work in the lower level stockroom. They'd knocked off for morning coffee break and were stretching it to lunchtime. Behind a stack of irregular carpet-slipper boxes, they were doing something with dice and eating deli.

Small amounts of money and tuna salad were changing hands. A shadow fell between their activities and the drop-cord light. It was Barnie's, and it spread far more than his five feet across the cement floor. "Say listen, you guys," he said in a voice cast as deep as possible, "my uncle up in the Executive Suite figured I might be able to give you a hand." Hands closed over dice. An extra tuna-salad sandwich was offered up.

Up in the Employees' Cafeteria Teresa pushed a tray past the steam table, following Dawn. Teresa passed up the sweating Jell-O, the cole slaw, the cucumbers in vinegar, and the prune danishes left over from coffee break. She checked out the meringue on the lemon cream pie, decided it looked tired, and went for the carrot cake with the cream-cheese icing.

The meat loaf looked edible, but the gray mushroom gravy was a definite downer. She moved in on the stuffed cabbage in creole sauce instead, holding up two fingers until the steam-table woman gave in and doubled the portion with a twitching spoon. The gravy on the mashed potatoes attacked her salivary glands, and so she ordered a double on them too, rounding off with sides of limas and three-bean salad. "I could eat a horse," she mentioned to Dawn.

"You might," Dawn grunted.

With a lunatic mind of its own, one of the cafeteria sprinkler spigots had cut loose right over the iced-tea vat, so everybody was going for the coffee. Dawn and Teresa found a table in the corner. Dawn surveyed her plate. "Would you look at this slop?"

Not remembering her last square meal, Teresa gripped a knife and fork, ready to plunge. She held back. "Anyhow, it's free."

"Typical Corporate American perversion of the Welfare State," Dawn explained.

But by then Teresa was shoveling up the limas. Food fueling her, she began to plan, trying to think in Dawn's patterns.

College kids, Teresa thought. Hard to figure. Big words. Simple minds. Old, but like babies still.

Still you got to start somewhere. "So, Dawn," Teresa said, trying not to grovel in gravy, "how's the career shaping up?"

"You kidding?" Dawn forked out a mushroom cap and deposited it on the table. "The first day it was Class-System-type putdowns from that merchandising trainee leader, who's a really uptight b—"

"That was yesterday," Teresa said. "How about today?"

"Don't rub it in. Drying dishes all morning? Listen," Dawn forked pimento bits ruthlessly out of the corn, "I never even dried dishes at *home*. You kidding?"

"Way I see it," Teresa said, improvising like mad, "today's a picnic compared with the usual routine. I mean you ought to be glad that sprinkler system went haywire."

"Get off my back," Dawn said, showing interest.

"Would I kid you? At least they have you working out in the open. You know Miss Filbert in Junior Miss?"

Dawn leaned a little across the table. "Old bag in the glasses."

"She's not that old actually," Teresa said. "It's just that they had her tagging merchandise in a stockroom for so long that it ruined her eyesight and put a lot of years on her."

"They had her doing nothing but tagging merchandise for *years*?" Dawn's fork fell across meat loaf. Her hands grasped the table edge.

"Six years." Teresa looked at the ceiling and seemed to calculate. "No, I'm lying to you. It was seven. Of course after that they gave her a raise."

Teresa's fork slid under a mountain of mashed potatoes. "You ought to get in with Miss Filbert," she said. "She might be able to knock a few years off stockroom for you if you can get her on your side."

Dawn looked like a drowning woman. Her face seemed to be turning inside out. "Listen, there's gotta be a union—"

"For merchandising trainees?" Teresa asked.

Dawn broke.

Her paper napkin fluttered down on her tray. She disappeared under the table, going for her shoulder-strap tote bag. She had it on her lap, and her chair was already scraping back. She was rummaging in the tote with mad, rushing fingers. "Here!" Dawn yelled, slamming her trainee's name tag on the table. "Give *that* to your uncle, you little . . . Capitalist Tool. And tell him to shove—"

But Dawn was already gone, stumbling between the tables, stalking and staggering out of the cafeteria, out of merchandising training.

Teresa laid a knife across her polished plate and reached for the name tag.

Ten floors down, on the lower level, the stockroom foursome had become a quintet. The boss's nephew, sent down from on high, had been outfitted from Popular Prices Workshirts & Wash Pants, straight off the unloading dock.

Barnie's small construction boots peeped out from under a pair of crisp gray twill pants, knife creased. On the flap pocket of his miniature work shirt the stock boys had clipped a laminated I.D. badge. On it the senior stockboy had lettered BARNIE LEDSMAR. They made quite a fuss over Barnie. He was the first contact they'd ever had with the Executive Suite. And Barnie, modest as ever, let them.

They'd have been happy to have him just hang out, as a mascot. But Barnie got busy. Even before the first customers poured in through the plywood doors upstairs in search of Amazing Reductions in Selected Water-Damaged Items, Barnie was setting a good example for the stock staff. He was razoring open cartons of slightly irregular pantyhose for Popular Prices and stacking flats of yogurt for Gourmet. There was a bustling new rhythm in the stockroom, and everybody found something to do.

Up on two Teresa, wearing Dawn's trainee name tag, found herself alone in Stemware. She fell to work, wringing out wet cloths into plastic buckets and sopping up the ponds in the Steuben Showcase. Getting good with the towels, she gave one a crack in the air and was just giving a special polish to a set of Waterford sherbets when the first customers hit Stemware.

"No reductions in this department," she explained firmly to a patron festooned with shopping bags. "Water just adds that little touch of sparkle to my stock. Interest you in anything at full price? My Fostoria begins at—" But the patron had lumbered off toward Tall Girls.

Some of the stemware was drying on its own. So Teresa gave herself a crash course on the cash register and boned up on brands and prices. She also kept an eye out for the stemware buyer, whoever that might be.

By midafternoon she'd sold a pair of bud vases and a punch bowl with matching cups, dried off the charge-plate gizmo, and ducked behind the wrap desk just as Bertha thundered by on the way to a collar.

Rising up from wrap, Teresa noticed the store intercom. She consulted a directory and dialed the lower level stockroom. The senior stock boy picked up on the first ring. "Stemware speaking," Teresa said in a voice more like Betty's. "Got a new fellow name of Barnie down there?"

"Yes . . . ma'am. Nice little fellow. Sent down from the Executive Suite—"

"That's right," Teresa said. "As long as you know." Then, thinking of some excuse for this call, she added, "Say listen, I may run short of packing boxes in Stemware, and I figure Gift Wrap on main's out of commission. You guys have any extra cartons, just in case I need them?"

"Yes, ma'am. All you want. You want me to send Barnie up with a supply?"

Teresa considered. "If I was you, I wouldn't work his tail off, if you know what I mean. Give you a call back later if I need you." She hung up, pretty satisfied that Barnie had found a happy home.

Teresa was still holding her own personal Early Warning alert for the stemware buyer. But the next person into the department was a customer, of sorts.

She was a little old woman with a nose veil and suspiciously large sleeves on a too winterish coat. Chees, Teresa thought, Fingers Ferguson at large already. She glided up to the grandmotherly soul who was eyeing a display of glass owl figurines. "Say, Fingers," Teresa said, kindly and quietly, "Bertha just went by, and it didn't look like a one-way trip. I'd make myself scarce if I were you."

Fingers' fingers rose to her neck, and her cheeks went chalky beneath the veil and blusher. Her mouth was firm

155

with outrage, but her eyes were grateful. She made a ladylike beeline for the Down escalator.

Since Teresa seemed to be the entire Stemware staff, she passed up afternoon coffee break. Instead she was rearranging to her own satisfaction a group display of pub mugs in rock crystal.

Crystal, Teresa thought, suddenly remembering the early morning battle. This is Crystal's Duty Station. Wonder where she takes cover? Teresa drifted back to the Stemware stockroom. Nothing there but an over-sized crate labeled FRAGILE up at the dry end. On a hunch she moved closer. The box was long enough all right, and there wasn't anything else around except open shelves. The top of the crate was sheared off. She leaned over the side, looking down into a mound of shredded paper. Working her way along to the end of the carton, she stuck her hand down through the shreds, reaching for the bottom.

A pair of dripping fangs sank into her palm. "Oh chees," Teresa said, "this is always happening."

She jerked her arm back in a shower of paper. There were two red puncture marks in the heel of her hand and a curve of tooth marks on the other side. "The phantom strikes again," Teresa muttered, "and enough's enough." She began throwing handfuls of paper out of the crate, slowing as she neared the bottom.

One final clump carefully removed uncovered Panty-hose. Her fur was studded with shreds. She turned a heart-shaped face up at Teresa, examining her with enormous yellow eyes heavy with sleep. The cat lay coiled tail-to-nose at the end of a pair of human feet.

"Crystal," Teresa said, and the shredded paper stirred.

"Is it A.C.T. yet?" the paper asked in a ghostly voice.

"Come out and see for yourself."

The paper parted, and Crystal sat up. The whole thing gave Teresa the creeps. Crystal's face still had an early morning look. Her only memorable feature was the small circle of her mouth. Her hair was a mess. She wore a canvas overall thing which might or might not be a stock girl's apron. On her it looked like a shroud. But what could you expect from somebody who lolled around all day in this crate-shaped coffin?

Crystal cocked her head and listened for distant sounds. "Why, it's still S.H., isn't it? It's still Store Hours!" Her head began to disappear into paper.

"Hold it!" Teresa said. Only Crystal's face reappeared on the surface. Teresa shook her head. "In your way, Crystal, you're weirder than Rosemary."

"Nobody's weirder than Rosemary," Crystal said. "And what are we doing rendezvousing during S.H. and right where I take cover too? It's craziness. What would Barbie—"

"Forget Barbie for two minutes," Teresa said. "Listen, where's the Stemware buyer? I'm all alone on the floor out there."

"She's in Czechoslovakia," Crystal said, as if any fool would know this.

"Czechoslovakia?"

157

"That's right. She's buying stemware from the Czechs. She's there till the end of the month. Wait a minute—" Crystal drew back, rustling paper, and her small round mouth formed a silent shriek. "That name tag—you're not one of us. You're a merchandising trainee! Dawn Botts! What kind of a name is that? You've blown my cover!" Crystal flung a fragile wrist up to the small circle of her mouth. Her eyes were aflame with fear. Even Pantyhose stood up on all four paws, looking concerned.

"Try to keep calm," Teresa said in a take-charge voice.

"But what—but who—" Crystal was shattered.

Teresa reached through paper to take a firm grip on her shoulder. "Climb on out of that box, and I'll tell you all about myself. And another thing, Crystal: during S.H. you're working for me."

chapter

sixteen

It was After Closing Time in a nearly dry store. The sound of the Sony drifted down to seven from eight, which meant that the nightwatchman and Pantyhose were drowsing in front of Tom Snyder.

In Beds & Bedding Teresa lay at attention under the queen-size, listening to Barnie's slight snore. He stirred suddenly. "What's that?" he said.

"What's what?"

"I thought I heard . . . something."

"Nothing yet," Teresa said. "But they'll be coming for us any minute now."

Ahead of them lay the Sentence. Teresa concentrated on reviewing the day instead.

The whole Stemware setup had gone like a Swiss

watch. And then at closing time she'd totaled up her cash drawer and handed over the take to some mouse from Accounting who hadn't even looked her in the eye. After that Teresa had followed the other sales personnel to clock out on Dawn's time card. She'd doubled back and made it to seven ahead of the sweepers and waited under the queen-size until Barnie'd crept up from the lower-level stockroom.

"You still awake, Barn?"

"Yeah. You still think we can beat the rap, Teresa?"

"Rap, schmap. We win on our terms or . . ."

"Or?"

"We win on our terms. Period."

Barnie seemed to be rubbing his forehead. To take his mind off things, Teresa said, "Glad you finally got rid of that lumber jacket. You smell a lot better."

Barnie stirred. "Listen, Teresa, you better remember those people have got us outnumbered. It's not just Barbie, you know. It's a big crowd. And you're not going to pull any sprinkler-system business on them."

"I—we been outthinking *and* outmaneuvering them all day, haven't we? Besides, there's always the unexpected which they tend to panic at and we don't."

"Still—"

"I know. But look, Barn. If they exon . . . exon—"

"Exonerate?"

"Yeah. They exonerate us, and then what? If we're Not Guilty, then what are we? One of them? Never. We're not like them. We're too—"

160

"Inner city?"

"Whatever. Besides, you *want* to be like them? Like Threads or Swank? Like *Scuba*?"

"You kidding? I got me a real job now, days. Maybe I'm not on the payroll, but who needs it? I got my uniform. We eat right out of Gourmet, even before Gourmet gets it. And I got a bed at night. So okay, I sleep under it. Still I got a bed."

"There you go, Barn. You're way ahead of them. And so am I. We got to stay ahead of them."

"True. But we also got to get through the night."

Through the night came the footfalls of four sock feet. They padded from the direction of Furniture & Furnishings, past Daybeds & Recliners, and entered Beds & Bedding, nearer and nearer the queen-size.

A finger raised the bedspread. A thumb, dimly outlined, gestured Barnie and Teresa out. They rolled into the aisle, at the feet of Ken and Threads.

It was a class act in a way. There was no binding or gagging. No hammerlocks, no Scuba threats. Just an escort. Ken, flannel all dry now and lightly scented with Old Spice, lifted Barnie to his feet as Threads reached for Teresa.

They moved off through the gloom, Ken just at Barnie's elbow and Threads at Teresa's, his eyes invisible beneath his hat brim. At the far end of Furniture & Furnishings he parted the first wall of curtains, and it fell closed behind the four of them. As the second pair began to open, Teresa had a minor inspiration and took

161

Threads's silken arm just to give Barbie something to think about. Threads quivered, but she snuggled closer.

Light struck their eyes, and they stepped onto white shag. Almost all of both shifts, yawning, were assembled in the vignette. Barbie was at her post behind the drop leaf, her little fist rapping for order almost soundlessly. Crystal from Stemware was trying frantically to whisper into her ear.

Barbie's glittering eyes narrowed to slits when she saw Teresa's casual hold on Threads. Crystal galloped from the drop leaf back to the semicircle and was whispering away like crazy to Betty.

And Betty was breathing, "*Not* . . . to . . . be . . . believed! Could you simply freak out?"

"I'll have order in here, or you'll all be in crates!" Barbie smiled desperately. "Prisoners to their knees!" She seemed to laugh delightedly, silently, but her hand was gripping the bow at her neck.

"I call this meeting to order." Barbie's golden curls seemed more tightly sprung than ever. "Threads! Get up here beside me. And I see no reason why our routine should be further disrupted just because there are two Prisoners here on Trial for their lives."

Threads loosed himself from Teresa and joined Barbie, who looked coldly through him, saying, "We have only a skeleton staff on Night Patrol. Who's reporting from them?"

"Butch from Sporting Goods and the Exercise Salon," Ken said quietly.

"Yes, well, come up, Butch, wherever you are."

Something mountainous rose up behind Teresa. She was back in her old kneeling position by Barnie, with a greatly expanded semicircle gathered behind her. Butch breezed by, smelling like a gym.

He stumbled over his Adidas on the way to the front. His small head rode atop a bull's body. A dank sweat shirt stretched across his bulging chest and flopped over a tiny waist.

"Well, it's like"—he piped in a high voice—"like the . . . ah . . . Mouth-Breathers are like . . ."

"Like what, Butch?" Madame Chairperson said impatiently. "What about the Mouth-Breathers?"

"Well," Butch struggled in a soprano voice, "it's like they're, you know . . . back."

"Bor-ring."

"Shut up, Betty. Now listen, Butch," Barbie urged, "try to make sentences when you talk. Then we'll know what you're saying."

Butch's arms, muscle-bound to uselessness, hung hopelessly. His wrists looked moist beneath the copper bracelets. He was trying to form words that were neither "like" nor "you know" and couldn't think of any.

"He's been here since fourth grade," someone muttered from the semicircle. "He's practically *illiterate*."

"Shut up out there," Barbie said. "Go on, Butch. The Mouth-Breathers are back in the parking lot, right?"

Butch nodded. "But it's like the county sheriff's car is like guarding the doors on their side. They've put up

163

like plywood ones because the glass ones got all broken by the firemen."

"Very good, Butch," Barbie said. "You're doing fine. Keep it rolling."

Butch struggled on. "Our best information is that they like all have court . . ."

"Court dates, Butch?"

"Yeah, like that. That won't slow them down much. But they'll probably keep out of the store for the . . . the . . ."

"Foreseeable future?" Barbie suggested.

Butch nodded gratefully, made a fist, and looked at it.

"Anything else to add, Butch?"

"Well," he squeaked, "our own Night . . . Patrol is, you know, making their rounds. But we're worn out. All that sleeping today kind of like shot us down. My own body"—he pointed at it—"feels, you know, *wiped out*." He hung his head and seemed to whimper.

"Very upsetting for you," Barbie said, moving forward and patting one of his biceps. "But you can go and sit down now.

"Which brings us," Barbie murmured, "back to our legal proceedings." Barnie was staring down past his I.D. tag to the spot of dried blood left by Swank on the shag.

"Last night's proceedings were interrupted, as we all know, by the Mouth-Breather invasion. This outrage was then interrupted by the sprinkler system. Which only goes to show that if we'd had a quicker jury decision, we wouldn't have to go over all this again, which is—"

"Bor-ring."

"Well, yes. But shut up, Betty."

"The question remains, are the so-called 'Teresa' and 'Barnie' Mouth-Breathers or aren't they?"

Draperies sighed, and Rosemary entered with a little skip. "Oh, definitely not!" she said, eyes darting.

"Late again, Rosemary," Madame Chairperson said. "What am I going to do with you?"

"Horsewhip me?" Rosemary asked hopefully.

"Oh, sit down and shut—"

"But no really," Rosemary was saying, all out of breath. "They can't be Mouth-Breathers. I have reason to know they're not—I mean my Heart Has Its Reasons." She lowered her purple lids a little. "Besides, they're not the type, quite. And, for another, it was Teresa who set off the sprinkler system. If she hadn't, I despair to think of our fate. Our tails would certainly have been in a wringer." Rosemary smiled dreamily and settled into the semicircle in a small sea of chiffon.

Teresa chanced a glance at Barnie, wondering if he was picking up the same signals she was. It was hard to say. He was only staring into the carpet, evidently looking for guidance.

"Scratch everything Rosemary said," Madame Chairperson spat. "I didn't give her permission to speak."

"We'd better stop scratching all over the place," Crystal said suddenly from the floor, "because Teresa is also Dawn Botts, who's a merchandising trainee and blew my cover and then put me to work drying stemware, which I didn't really mind, and she's absolutely in charge of the department during S.H., and she *can be too* because the buyer's in Czechoslovakia and—"

"Sergeants-at-arms!" Barbie blurted out. "Seize her! She's babbling. One more outburst from you, Crystal, and I'll have you in a crate."

"Actually," Crystal said, "I wouldn't mind all that much. I spend half the time in one anyway. At least I did before Teresa—I mean Dawn—"

"Oh, shut up, Crystal. I'll think of something else to do to you." Barbie's Cupid's-bow mouth was beginning to droop. Something very uncute was creeping into her face. She knew Crystal wasn't babbling. She'd understood every word. "I've had it up to here with all this Freedom of Speech and Trial by Jury and like that.

"I'll deliver a verdict on these two—especially her"— Barbie darted a look down at Teresa—"and I won't horse around all night doing it either." Barbie drew herself up. "I don't care if 'Teresa' did or didn't set off the sprinkler system, and I'm not interested in her motives. One thing nobody around here but me has picked up on is that the Mouth-Breathers invaded on the *very night* we apprehended these two. I'd think that coincidence would blow all your minds, if you had any."

"*Actually*," said Betty, "it wasn't all that much of a coincidence. After all Teresa and Barnie had already been in the store for an extended period before we collared them. I mean, *really*, Mouth-Breathers are *superb* at mugging and vandalism and the more gross-type behavior. But did you ever hear of any of them surviving in the store during S.H. and then taking cover and like that? It's miles too subtle for Mouth-Breathers."

"I've abolished the jury, Betty," Madame Chairperson said. "You're out of order."

"B—"

"I'm simply too confused," said a girl with bright red cheeks, pigtails, and a baby's voice. It was Dolly from Toys on five. "Even though I'm Gifted, I can't handle it when two different ideas come down in my space."

"Oh shut up, Dolly."

"No, I don't want to."

Teresa hazarded a sidelong look at her. Dolly's voice went with her pigtails, but not her bust, which was enormous. "I mean Crystal says Teresa's a merchandising trainee. Right? And you say she's a Mouth-Breather. I'm Gifted, but honestly I can't get a handle on this." Dolly drew a large breath and pouted it out, drawing a lot of attention.

Barbie's eyes were narrowing again. The group was growing restless. There was that breeze-through-trees sound again, and it was noticeable now. "Dolly, you'll just have to stay confused because there's nobody here who can tell us who and what the so-called 'Teresa' and 'Barnie' are." Barbie even managed the ghost of a smile.

"I can."

167

It was Teresa speaking. She was climbing to her feet. Ken wavered over her, uncertain. "I can and will," she said in a voice dangerously loud.

"Prisoners don't speak in their own defense," Barbie remarked. "It's a rule. One of my own." Threads was rounding the drop leaf and bearing down on Teresa.

"Lay one finger on me, sucker," she told him in a mutter, "and I'll rip that silk blouse right off you." Threads shrank.

"I'm nobody's prisoner," she said, practically booming it out, "and neither is Barnie here. Get up, Barnie. Sit down, Ken, unless you're afraid of bending your blazer." Teresa turned to the group, blotting Barbie out.

"As far as you turkeys are concerned, my identity happens to be one Dawn Botts." She flicked her trainee name tag. "I'm as good as a store employee. I sent the real Dawn Botts packing, and when the Stemware buyer comes back, I'll be Dawn Botts permanently. If you think I can't pull that off, hide and watch. I intend to wear stockings and heels. And, by the way, I'd like you to meet my friend here from the lower-level stockroom. If you can read, you'll see from his I.D. badge who *he* is."

"Oh whoops!" said Dolly. She was leaning forward to read. "Barnie *Ledsmar.*"

"A true identity revealed!" sighed Rosemary. "How fatally romantic."

Barbie, shaken but still practical, threw herself across the drop leaf and made a grab for Teresa's sleeve. "For heaven's sake, at least keep that honking inner-city voice of yours down. The nightwatchman's asleep, but he's not *dead*."

"Do I care?" Teresa wanted to know. "I and my friend here are a couple of legitimate store personnel as of today. We can yell the place down if we feel like it. And, by the way, if we don't turn up for work tomorrow, we'll be missed."

"It's true, it's true," Crystal moaned in a sort of pleased anguish, "every word."

Teresa continued. "We're a couple of bona fide store employees who happened to work late and discovered a pack of runaway, truant, cream-puff kids freeloading off Forbes and Ledsmar. *That* ought to make interesting reading in your favorite local Suburban Weekly."

Feeling cautiously pleased with herself, Teresa let that sink in.

But Barbie's voice knifed into the stunned silence. She'd edged around the table where she'd be visible again. "Being broadminded, I can maybe imagine a pair of Mouth-Breathers might be just Gifted enough to infiltrate both *us* and the Store Personnel. This, of course, was a couple of Independent Acts, which are both felonies. But I'm willing to overlook that."

She patted her golden curls in the old way, dredged up a winning smile, and said, "I find 'Teresa' and 'Barnie' Guilty on the Amended Charge of being Gifted Mouth-Breathers who committed one other Crime which has not come to light."

She had the whole group in the palm of her hand

169

again. They really responded to Guilty verdicts. Teresa was about half ready to call it quits and sink to her knees.

"The Mouth-Breather strike force got into this store *without* breaking in at the parking-lot entrance, which would of course have tripped the alarm system right away. Am I right, Swank?"

Swank agreed through split lips.

"But they got in here some other way. Maybe the unloading dock or any other entrance 'Teresa' or 'Barnie' left open for them. So these two are Guilty because I say so."

The semicircle shifted uneasily and edged a little toward Barbie. She was doing their thinking for them again, and it felt good. Dolly looked relieved and tried to hug herself a little. Madame Chairperson, back in the saddle again, basked in their approval a moment too long.

Rosemary rose like a ghost out of the group. Her bird face was white as death. Her eyes were fluttering, and she was whispering to herself, "Courage, give me courage."

Out loud she said, "Madame Chairperson, Prisoners, members of the jury—"

"I've already *abolished* the jury, Rosemary, if you'd only *listen*." Barbie's hand raked her curls.

"I have a confession to make," Rosemary said, "and then I'm going to throw myself on the mercy of the court or whatever."

"Is this fact or fiction, Rosemary?" Betty asked. "Because *honestly* I think we ought to know whether you're acting out one of your little fantasies again or not."

"Fact," said Rosemary firmly. Everyone stared at her. Even Barnie shifted around.

"Teresa and Barnie aren't Mouth-Breathers. And they didn't let the Mouth-Breathers in. I was responsible for that."

No one spoke, but everyone believed her. It didn't sound a bit like Rosemary. It sounded real. Threads and Ken moved toward her. "I'm not a Mouth-Breather," Rosemary said, much too sanely, "but I have a friend who is, a friend of my *own*." Her eyes glowed with doomed pride.

"No you haven't," Barbie snapped. "We don't make friends with Mouth-Breathers. The situation doesn't arise. There can be no friendships between two gangs— I mean a group and a gang.

"Besides," Barbie went on, "*we're* your friends, Rosemary. And the only friends you'll ever have."

"Oh, no." Rosemary was shaking her head. "I have a Mouth-Breather friend. I've had her for quite a long time, and none of you even knew it. And she doesn't boss me around or think I'm . . . strange, or anything. I don't mind being the misfit in this group as long as I can be me with someone else."

"And where is the little worm?" Barbie inquired.

"She's down in the Book Department where we spend a lot of time together. I showed her how to take cover and everything."

"You *didn't*," Betty gasped, gripping her suede vest.

171

"I did so," Rosemary said. "I even take her food sometimes, though she boosts on her own in Gourmet. She's down in the Book Department this very minute, lying along the back of that long shelf of Judy Blumes."

"Sergeants-at-arms! Go down there and look behind the Judy Blumes and see if there's a Mouth-Breather there. And get the lead out of your pants!"

The semicircle churned, and Threads and Ken leaped into action, colliding with each other.

"Oh, no, you mustn't," Rosemary said. "You might frighten her. I'll go get her. Besides, she might be behind the Nancy Drews. She's not much of a reader."

"And what if you don't come back?" Barbie asked, drumming the table ominously.

"Then your group here, Barbie, will be just a little drabber." Rosemary moved through the curtains with immense dignity.

Just then Julia appeared from the dining vignette and said softly, "I have an *acre* of meat loaf in mushroom sauce and enough lemon meringue pie and ice tea for everybody, and if you don't all come on and eat it this minute, I'm going to throw it out because you know all that stuff leaves odors."

The entire semicircle turned on her and hissed, "Shut up, Julia!" Even Teresa and Barnie.

chapter
seventeen

Teresa never quite remembered the exact moment when Barbie stopped being Madame Chairperson. She'd been lured away from the drop leaf when Teresa stood up and started shooting off her mouth. Then when Rosemary dropped *her* bombshell, Barbie was practically part of the semicircle.

Now, while everybody waited for Rosemary to come back, Barbie seemed about to wilt onto the floor like anybody else. It'd been so easy to be the leader when everybody obeyed, but now things were so difficult. And it was clear to Teresa that Barbie had never experienced difficulties before.

Her lips had lost their lacquer, and her curls seemed to be unraveling. There was hardly anything cute about her. Her little fists were as limp as Butch's big ones.

Their table-pounding nights were over. Ken and Threads, somewhat faithful to the end, led her away and dropped her at the back of the semicircle.

There was nobody up there behind the drop leaf, and everybody avoided looking at the empty place of power. Everybody but Teresa.

She watched Barnie scan the room, a prisoner no longer. No Mouth-Breather rap hung over them now that there was a living, breathing Mouth-Breather shelved in Books.

Everything seemed different to Teresa. The furniture in the vignette looked bigger, and every human form looked smaller. People picked nervously at the white shag. Light from a table lamp cast hollow shadows across cheeks.

Propped up against an end table, a kid smaller than Barnie sat slumped, wearing only Fruit of the Loom underwear with the labels showing. It was an unusual, pathetic sight. Teresa focused on the guy's little weasel face and saw it was Scuba.

Just at that moment Barnie said, "Hey, Scube, where's your wet suit?"

Scuba looked terrified and drew up minute knees. His face turned a deep maroon, but he had to answer. People were looking. "My wet suit got wet . . . when the sprinklers went off."

Betty made a very sophisticated clicking sound with her teeth. "He *wet* his wet suit when he got one look at those Mouth-Breathers pouring into main," Betty said. "Could you simply puke?"

174

Scuba's head dipped below his knees, but Barnie had broken the ice. Everyone was talking now, quietly. Even people who never talked, and all of them without permission. From the back, Barbie groaned.

The curtains parted. Rosemary stepped just inside, looking serious and a little bit pretty in an unearthly way. She stood there until every eye was on her. Then she reached back through the curtains and drew forth the Mouth-Breather.

"Oh honestly!" Betty grasped her Harris tweed. "Remember miniskirts?"

The Mouth-Breather tried to shelter behind Rosemary, but she was somewhat larger all around. Gently Rosemary led her into the light. The Mouth-Breather wouldn't look up. She'd fixed her stare on one of Rosemary's chiffon scarves. Her free hand dangled down past the miniskirt, and her fingers ended in five knobs.

"Oh dear, a nail biter," Julia sighed. "Unsanitary. But you can get those false ones that shape."

"Oh looky," Dolly said, "what's that spelled out on her T-shirt in nailheads?"

Butch squinted forward and tried to read the T-shirt and couldn't.

"It says Sha-Na-Na Forever," Betty said, more in pity than anything else.

"She has a skin condition," Crystal noted, "but nothing that couldn't be helped by Medicated Cosmetics down on main."

From under his hat brim Threads said something about shampoo.

"With a basic tailored blouse," Barbie said, strictly as one of the group, "and maybe some good French jeans to cover up those legs . . ."

And still Rosemary stood there, holding the Mouth-Breather by the hand. "When you're all finished trying to make somebody completely over until she's just like the rest of you," she said quietly, "I'd like to introduce you to my friend, Agnes."

"Agnes?" Scuba's head popped up over his bare knees. "What kind of a name is Agnes?"

"Her own," Teresa said to Scuba. "What's yours?"

It must have been then when everybody started looking to Teresa, even though she didn't take up a position behind the drop leaf. She was on her feet to greet the newcomer while everybody else just sat there. "How's it going, Agnes?"

It looked as if Agnes's grip was shutting off the circulation in Rosemary's hand, but she managed to meet Teresa's gaze. She had a permanently dazed look, having no eyebrows. She'd lost them in her early Mouth-Breather days when she fell off the back of a Suzuki onto a gravel road. With nothing much above her eyes and Rosemary beside her with violently violet lids, the two of them looked like a single face trying to come together. There were also permanent burn scars on Agnes's calves from Kawasaki exhaust pipes. There was no doubt that she mistook Teresa for the Madame Chairperson she'd heard so much about from Rosemary. Her tongue had gone dead in her mouth.

"Come on, Agnes," Teresa said kindly, "this bunch

here thinks Mouth-Breathers only grunt. Haul off and prove them wrong."

Agnes's browless eyes flickered with a little cautious light. This wasn't exactly what she'd expected from Madame Chairperson. "There is some grunting," Agnes managed to say, "but we talk."

She paused and realized she had the floor. "We're not *big* talkers," she went on, warming up a bit. "I mean we were all in the slower classes in school, and they don't give you much after they've stuck you in them. Once they've pegged you, they've pegged you for life." Agnes fell silent and seemed to be reading Sha-Na-Na Forever upside down.

"School, you say?" Teresa said, feeling the tension around her feet. "If you've been anywhere near school lately, you're way ahead of this group. Right, Butch?" She whirled around to where he sat between his enormous wrists. Butch cowered.

"Look, Agnes," Teresa continued, "correct me if I'm wrong. You probably grew up in this Mouth-Breather outfit, but you're out of the grease pit now or you wouldn't have teamed up with Rosemary. Am I right?"

Agnes nodded and tugged a little at the hem of her miniskirt, which was plastic. "It was the only thing going in my neighborhood," she said quietly, "but they had me on hubcaps forever, and you could go blind from all that black leather."

"I see your point," Teresa said. "There's no growth in a gang." Teresa's eyes swept over the semicircle. "This bunch here is exhibit A on that. Give me one good

177

friend you can really trust any old day. I got a good friend. Barnie, here." Barnie waved a small hand at Agnes. And Agnes worked up her first smile.

A voice from the semicircle murmured, "She could use some orthodonture, but basically—"

"Knock it off, Betty," Teresa said. "But listen, Agnes, I got no business prying into your private life. The thing of it is, this bunch wants to find out how the Mouth-Breathers got into the store. You let them in, Agnes? Leave a door unlocked, something like that?"

Agnes closed her eyes, which left the entire top half of her face a blank. Rosemary's arm must have been numb to the shoulder. Agnes nodded.

"We can handle *one* of them," said Threads. "Slap the living—"

Teresa rounded on him. "And I can handle you, Threads. You can bet your plated-gold chains on that." Silence fell.

"Go on, Agnes. Nobody's going to lay a finger on you. Just tell it."

"Priscilla made me do it," Agnes said. "She's the Honcho. I always looked up to Priscilla and thought she was a really together lady."

"Hold it a second, Agnes," Barnie said. "Is Priscilla a tall, rangy skateboarder wired for sound? She set you up to infiltrate the store?"

Agnes nodded. "She even outfitted me in these clothes so I wouldn't be conspicuous."

Betty looked faint.

"Of course," Agnes continued, "when I got in the

store, I saw I was all wrong. I knew I didn't fit in. I mean every stitch on me came from a Price Slashing at Discount-o-rama. But then I met Rosemary one day in that Nostalgia Boutique place. I didn't understand those clothes either. And I didn't understand Rosemary at first. But I really got to like her. She's not pushy or anything, and she isn't into power trips. Besides, everybody's a little bit weird. It's only normal."

Rosemary gave a little birdlike nod and smiled modestly.

"But they were always leaning on me," Agnes said. "The Mouth-Breathers. I couldn't even go near the parking lot. And one of the window trimmers who works in this store is an ex-Mouth-Breather."

"An ex-Mouth-Breather actually working here?" Crystal gasped.

"That's right," Agnes said. "He was thrown out of the gang for unmacho behavior, but he keeps in touch. *He* wouldn't leave a door unlocked because he had his job to think of, but he could sure send me plenty of threats from Priscilla. So I just slipped a little and went back to my old Mouth-Breather ways. It's always easier to do what you're told, isn't it?"

The vignette was so quiet then that Agnes went on to fill up the silence. "So I managed to deactivate the alarm on the unloading-dock door and loosen the screws on the lock. Then I—what do you people call it?— rendezvoused with Priscilla in the parking lot and told her which entrance. Then I felt really rotten. Oh, not because the Mouth-Breathers wanted to come in and wipe up the place with you people. I felt rotten because I'd sort of sold out Rosemary who's the only friend I ever had. So I don't care much what you do to me now. I been pounded on before."

Agnes shrugged. She seemed to have run down, but she hadn't quite. "Anyhow, the Mouth-Breathers'll be back. They'll find a way. Priscilla will see to that. How else could she keep her command? Wherever there's two gangs, there's going to be bloodshed. It's the name of the game. And it's too bad because they're just kids, and you're just kids. And what does it prove?"

It was so quiet then that the Sony up on eight could be heard playing "The Star Spangled Banner." It was getting late, practically morning. And everything that had been was no more. Even the vignette looked flimsier than before.

Teresa looked out over the store people. Scuba's hands were locked around his bare knees, and he was rocking himself back and forth. Dolly pulled a pigtail across her mouth and seemed to be sucking her thumb under it. Threads fingered his neck chains. Rosemary was no doubt thinking of castles, but they were all in the air. Swank's split lip looked black and crusty. Julia was doubtless thinking about the meat loaf and deciding it didn't much matter. Barnie's hand was unconsciously resting over his laminated badge and his heart because the national anthem was still playing.

Teresa waited. It was Barbie who finally spoke, a Barbie the rest of them had never known. "I want to go home," she said, "more than anything."

180

She struggled to her knees. "I don't want to be here anymore. The only reason I ever came here in the first place was I was mad at my mother, and I thought she'd really suffer if I disappeared. And I don't even know if she *did* suffer. She may not even have called the police or reported me missing or *anything*. I mean, did any of you ever see a *Wanted* poster on me? I've wondered for the longest time, and it simply drives me crazy. I bet Mother didn't suffer a *minute*."

Barbie had the floor for the last time and didn't even notice. Her voice was breaking all over the place, and the tears were streaming down her face. But the others didn't look down on her or up to her. They were all staring into the shag, looking at lives of their own.

Betty was rising now. She gave her suede vest and her knee socks little jerks. "Frankly," she said, brittle still, but sincere, "I was never really the President of the Student Council at my school. I lost by a landslide, and I didn't have the guts to face anybody. I'd done all the right things. I'd worn all the right things. I was just Gifted enough. But the truth is, I never was really popular." She stood there, swaying, but the mouth that had spoken truth was no longer a hard little line.

Butch heaved himself up and loomed over the group. "Like it was different for me," he piped. "My folks used to drop me off at the shopping mall every morning and leave me all day. It was like a big free baby-sitter, you know? One night they never came back for me. Maybe they moved away. Maybe there's some kind of a Bureau of Missing Parents I could check with."

They were all rising to their feet now. There was no reason to be quiet anymore, and yet nobody made much noise. People helped other people to their feet. Dolly brushed paper shreds off Crystal, who was softly sobbing. Threads helped Julia untie her apron and eased it off over her head. Her spatula fell to the floor among feet. In ones and twos several people lost in thought slipped off to the places where they hid their shoes.

Ken shrugged out of his blazer and covered Scuba with it. And then he said, "If my folks think about me at all, they think I'm at boarding school. Andover, actually. Maybe I ought to be." He cocked an eyebrow and reached across Barbie to shake Threads's hand. And then he walked to the curtains.

Everyone watched the back of his neck where blond hair waved down to the collar while he found the drapery cord and drew back the curtains. First the inner ones and then the outer.

Furniture & Furnishings stretched out before them. Conversational Modules stood speechless. And beyond, Daybeds & Recliners, and beyond that, Beds & Bedding and the entire seventh floor, and the world filling up with morning.

Pantyhose was just coming down the Up escalator, planting paws on the new day.

Teresa saw it all through eyes blurry with sleepiness and something else.

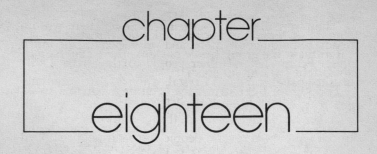

chapter eighteen

At nine thirty, three electronic chimes on a timer sounded to start the Forbes & Ledsmar day.

Strolling across the main floor beside Barnie, Teresa saw a shifty-eyed window trimmer in leather Levi's fastening the final bra on a swim-wear display.

She lingered at the top of the escalator to the lower level and gave Barnie the thumbs-up sign as he descended to the stockroom—off to a day's work and then an undisturbed night, for once, under the queen-size.

Then, just before the panzer division of early shoppers attacked from every entrance, she watched a different group coming down the escalator in a long file.

None of the sales personnel—except Teresa—appeared to notice them. If you didn't look too close, they seemed to be a new crop of merchandising trainees.

Plunging in to work late, Miss Filbert caught a dim glimpse of them and darted in another direction.

On main the group headed against the traffic pattern toward the parking-lot doors.

Parking-lot light struck the brim of a Panama straw hat. And it glowed in the gash of a split lip. A well-cut blazer exited on small bare legs far beneath the shoppers' eye level. The first of the parking lot's exhaust fumes enveloped tightly sprung golden curls. And behind pigtails an enormous bust inhaled air climate uncontrolled.

A tweedy girl in knee socks cast a backward look at the Smoking Is a No-No sign, tossed her head, said, "Bor-ring," and strode out.

Teresa watched until they were all out of sight. She knew it was scary for them all, walking off that way, with no leadership but themselves. But they were readier than they expected to commit a few Independent Acts.

A final three filed past her. Rosemary, she'd found out, was the daughter of the juvenile court judge. And Crystal's father was superintendent of schools. And both Agnes's parents were guidance counselors. So when Rosemary and Crystal and Agnes got home, Teresa figured they wouldn't even have been missed.

Teresa turned, then, and strode through knots of tussling shoppers, fighting over Amazing Reductions in Slightly Water-Damaged Goods. She had a big day ahead of her in Stemware. A whole career, in fact, unfurled before her as she started up the Up escalator.

Where do you go from merchandise trainee, she wondered. Head of the department, finally, she figured. Yes, Teresa thought, I'll be buying stemware in Czechoslovakia one day.

Might even drop a card to my aunt too. Invite her out to Paradise Park to take advantage of my ten-percent discount. And if I know anything about Barnie, he'll probably end up with the Employees' Award for Perfect On-Time Attendance in the stockroom.

The future looked pretty good from where Teresa stood, rising every minute on the escalator, up to Stemware on two.